O9-ABF-312

3 5086 00373585 7

THE SHATTERED STONE

THE SHATTERED STONE

by Robert Newman

illustrations by John Gretzer

Atheneum · New York · 1975

Chadron State College Library
Chadron, Nebraska

For Gabriel Samrock

Library of Congress Cataloging in Publication Data
Newman, Robert, 1909-
The shattered stone.
SUMMARY: *Neva and Ivo emerge from an enchanted place in the forest to meet many dangers, right a great wrong, and, hopefully, bring peace to two warring kingdoms.*
I. Gretzer, Robert. II. Title.
PZ7.N4857Sh [Fic] 75-6834
ISBN 0-689-30481-1

Copyright © 1975 by Robert Newman
All rights reserved
Published simultaneously in Canada by
McClelland & Stewart, Ltd.
Manufactured in the United States of America
By Book Press, Brattleboro, Vermont
Designed by Mary Ahern and Kathy Westray
First Edition

+
N 467s

Prologue

As he spoke the final words of the spell, he put out the last candle and the darkness became absolute. There was silence for a moment, and the room became chill with the cold of the void that lies beyond the stars. Then, in the darkness, an even blacker darkness stirred, and from it came a voice that was strangely and frighteningly quiet.

"If you have called me here lightly that will be your bane," it said.

"Since you know all," he answered, "you must know that it is not done lightly."

"Ah, yes. You want my help. But why should I give it to you?"

"Because, having learned enough of the forbidden

arts to summon you, I also know something of the great struggle you are engaged in—not only here but everywhere. And I think it would be to your purpose to aid me."

"Think you a kingdom—even a world—means aught in the battle I wage?"

"I do. And far less than that. So exactly poised are the scales that even a single life can shift the balance."

"You have learned much and learned it well."

"Then you will do it?"

"Yes. But knowing so much you must also know that there are laws that govern what I can do as there are what you can do. Exceed the established limits—use your powers directly—and you call into play countervailing forces."

"I know."

"You shall have my help then—under set conditions and for a time."

"What conditions and for how long a time?"

"Let us say twice ten years. If you have accomplished your ends in that time, there will be a place for you at my side through all eternity. But you know what the price will be if you fail."

"My life."

"Your life and more than your life. Well?"

He hesitated, weighing the risk against his consuming desire. Then as the darkness stirred again, coiling and thickening impatiently,

"It is agreed," he said.

THE FOREST

Chapter 1

Later in the day it would be quite warm; as warm as it ever got there in the green shade of the forest. But at the moment the air was fresh and cool and the dew hung gleaming on the grass, wetting their feet as they walked up the path from the hut to the cave.

A spider—one of the large ones whose threads Mistress Silvia used in her weaving—had spun a web across the path, and they paused in front of it. It would probably be broken before long by one of the animals who went this way to the pond, but neither Neva nor Ivo wanted to do so. Neva bent down, slipping under it, and Ivo followed her, trailing his staff.

They were going around the pond when Ronno,

the fox, appeared out of the underbrush. It was fairly clear that he had been outside, probably raiding one of the farms that lay a few miles from the forest, for he looked full and quite pleased with himself, and besides there was a chicken feather on his smooth red coat.

"Greetings," he said. "On your way to Mistress Silvia's?"

"Yes," said Neva.

"Too bad. It's a nice morning—too nice to spend sitting in one place."

"We don't mind," said Ivo. "Where have you been?"

"Nowhere in particular."

"Nowhere?" said Neva picking the chicken feather off his back and holding it up.

"I can't imagine how that got there," said Ronno, grinning. "What will you be learning today?"

"We never know," said Ivo. "It depends on our questions."

"I hope it's not monsters again," said Neva.

"Why?" asked Ivo. "So far we've always been able to handle them."

"I'm just getting a little tired of them. Besides I've never been really sure . . ."

There was a rumbling roar and a particularly horrible one appeared some distance up the path. It had three heads and a greenish body covered with scales. And though its huge, batlike wings were outstretched, it was not flying but running towards them, eyes blazing and jaws open.

They immediately took their defensive stance, turning sideways and raising their left fists, their right hands back with the forefinger pointing down.

With a baffled scream, the monster rose into the air over their heads and disappeared. Ivo picked up his staff and looked around for Ronno, but he had slipped away into the bushes.

"Strange," he said.

"What is?"

"That one of them should have appeared just when we were talking about them. What were you saying?"

"That I was getting tired of them?"

"No. Something else."

"Oh. Lately I've been wondering if they were real."

Ivo looked at her thoughtfully, then went a few paces up the path and bent down. There was no sign of the monster's claws in the soft earth and none of the bushes on either side of the path had been broken.

"I never thought of that," he said. "And you may be right. I think I'll make that one of my questions. Do you have all yours?"

"Yes."

"You always have," he said with admiring resignation.

They went on up the path and through the oaks that surrounded the glade. On its far side was the rocky hill with the cave at its base. Mistress Silvia sat just inside the entrance working at her loom.

"Good morning, mistress," they said.

"Good morning, children. You're late today."

"I had to help Jartan chop wood," said Ivo. "Then we met Ronno and a monster."

Mistress Silvia nodded, and Ivo sensed that she already knew all that just as she knew everything that happened in the forest.

"Who begins today?" she asked.

"I think I do," said Ivo. "Was the monster we met real?"

"Why do you ask?"

"Because Neva said she wasn't sure it was. And though it was very big and should have been very heavy, I couldn't find any signs of it after it was gone."

"No," said Mistress Silvia. "It wasn't real."

"Then why did we have to protect ourselves against it?"

"Why do you think?"

"I'm not sure. Because one day we may meet one that is real, and we should be ready for it?"

"Exactly."

"Then there are monsters like that one or like some of the others we've seen?"

"Would there be any need to be prepared for them if there weren't?"

"No."

"You have one more question."

He hesitated. He often had trouble thinking of the three questions with which they always began.

"When we met Ronno, he had been outside," he said, "probably stealing chickens at one of the farms. We know that there can be no killing here in this part of the forest. But isn't it just as wrong for him to kill out there?"

"Can you answer that, Neva?" said Mistress Silvia.

"I think so," said Neva. "And I don't think it's wrong."

"Why not?"

"Because Ronno can't live on the things that we eat. And besides it's part of his nature to hunt and kill."

"And that is something that cannot be changed," said Mistress Silvia. "Nor should it be. All we can ask of him is that he observe our laws here. Your questions today were not very searching, Ivo."

"I'm sorry."

"So you say most mornings, but you don't do much about it. If you thought about your questions a bit more, it would not take quite so long for you to learn the things that you must learn."

"And what must we learn?"

"You can make that one of your questions tomorrow. Now what are yours, Neva?"

Before Neva could answer, Sim, the bear cub, came shambling into the glade. When he saw Neva and Ivo, he broke into a galloping run, leaped into Ivo's lap, then off again and into Neva's, nuzzling her face when she hugged him.

"News, Neva," he squealed. "Wonderful news! I'm to have some honey!"

"Oh?" she said, rubbing his round, furry stomach. "Who said so?"

"Why, my mother. Didn't you, mother?" he asked Dahga who had paused at the edge of the glade.

"Forgive us, my lady," said Dahga. "I didn't know that Neva and Ivo were here."

"You should have. They're here every day at this time," said Mistress Silvia. "What's this about honey?"

"Some of Jartan's bees have swarmed and moved to the dead willow on the far side of the pond. But when we came near it, they threatened us."

"They said they'd sting me," said Sim. "On the nose."

"And what do you want me to do about it?"

"I haven't had any honey since last fall. And Sim's never even tasted it. I thought, if you sent them a message . . ."

"What do you say to that, Neva?" asked Mistress Silvia.

"The bees will have all summer to build up their store. I think that Dahga and Sim should be allowed to take some."

"Very well," said Mistress Silvia. "Tell them I said so. But you're to take only a little, not empty the hive."

"Yes, my lady. And thank you."

"Yes, thank you," said Sim, jumping off Neva's lap and running to her.

"You're welcome, Sim," said Mistress Silvia, stroking his head. Then as he and Dahga moved off, Sim bouncing with excitement, she turned to Neva again. "You were going to ask your questions."

"Yes," said Neva. "I don't know if this is one of the forbidden ones, but . . . Could I remember another place besides this?"

"There are no forbidden questions. There are just some I will not answer. But why do you ask that?"

"Because of a dream I had last night. I was somewhere else—a large room, much larger than my room in the hut. There was a woman with me. I could not see her face, but I knew it was not you. And I wondered if it was a dream or a memory."

"What do you think, Ivo?"

"I've sometimes wondered about the same thing because I've dreamed about other places, too. But I think it was because of what Jartan has told us about what lies outside the forest."

"It's unlikely that it was a memory, Neva," said Mistress Silvia. "Thinking back, what is the first thing you remember?"

"Being bathed in front of the fire in the hut," said Neva. "You were bathing me, but Jartan was there, too. And I think Ivo was there also."

"That's quite possible. And you, Ivo, what is the first thing you remember?"

"I think standing at the edge of the forest, looking at the heath and trying to get out on to it and finding I couldn't."

"That's possible, too. You were a wanderer from the time you could first walk. What's your next question, Neva?"

"It's one I've asked before and you wouldn't answer. Will we ever leave here?"

"It's what I thought you'd ask. Do you want to leave here?"

"Yes. Not for good, of course. Just for a while."

"Why?"

"Because Ivo has often said he'd like to go. And if he does, I want to go with him."

"Then you want to leave here, Ivo?"

"Yes, my lady. As Neva said, not for good. We would come back to you and Jartan."

"It might not be easy to come back. Why do you want to go?"

"I'd like to see some of the places Jartan has told us about—cities, mountains, other people."

"I think that one day you will go."

"When?" asked Neva.

"That is your third question?"

"Yes."

"How old are you, Neva?"

Neva and Ivo looked at one another. If anyone knew, Mistress Silvia did. They knew themselves because each year, on Midsummer Eve, Jartan stood them against one of the doorposts of the hut and made a mark to see how much they had grown. But since Mistress Silvia did few things without a reason, she must have had a reason for asking.

"This will be my seventeenth summer," said Neva.

Nodding, Mistress Silvia turned and wrote with her finger on the smooth stone at the side of the cave. She wrote not in the characters she had first taught them, but using the ancient Tree alphabet. The letters glowed faintly, and they read:

"You will go when you wish to go for the right reason."

She passed her hand over the stone, and the writing disappeared.

"And what is the right reason?" asked Ivo.

"You will have to discover that for yourselves. Now I have something for you." Reaching behind her, she brought out a basket of mushrooms. "Would you like these for your supper?"

Neva looked at them. There were three or four different kinds of mushrooms in the basket, none like any she had ever seen before.

"No, thank you, my lady."

"Why not?"

"Because they're poisonous."

"How do you know?"

"I just do."

"What say you, Ivo?"

Neva had always been quicker at this than he. He

had to take the mushrooms out one by one, look at them closely and smell them. But finally he said, "I think they're poisonous, too."

"Very good. What about these?" And she brought out another basket filled with morels, the most delicious of all wild mushrooms.

"We would like those," he said.

"Then take them. You can go now. Neva will stay here with me for a while."

"Yes, my lady," he said. "Thank you."

Picking up the basket of morels, he started across the glade. When he reached the oaks on the far side, he glanced back. Mistress Silvia and Neva were sitting close to one another, looking alike and yet unalike; both wearing tunics of shimmering grey spider silk, both with their hair long and hanging loose around their shoulders. But while Mistress Silvia's hair was dark, Neva's was tawny, gleaming with red and coppery lights. And though Mistress Silvia's lovely, ageless face was calm and grave, Neva's was intent as if she were listening to something.

Mistress Silvia began working at her loom again, and Ivo went on along the path. He wondered, as he had before, what they did when he was not there. He had asked Neva, and all she would say was that Mistress Silvia was teaching her things she felt were important. That seemed only right when he thought about it, for after all Jartan had taught him many things that he had not taught Neva.

Ivo paused for a moment at the edge of the pond. A kingfisher was hovering over the deep part near the bank. Suddenly it dived, disappearing completely. But when it bobbed to the surface, its long bill was empty, and with an angry cry of "Damned trout!" it flashed off. Ivo smiled. It was quite warm now, and he was tempted to go for a swim. But, as with most things, it was more fun to do that with Neva than alone so he moved on.

As he came into the clearing, he heard the sound of Jartan's axe and knew that he must still be chopping wood. Putting the basket of morels inside the hut, he walked around to the side of it with his staff over his shoulder.

"I'm back, Jartan," he said.

Jartan, tall and grey-bearded, was standing over a log and just raising his axe. As Ivo approached, he turned suddenly and struck at him. Sliding his hands apart, Ivo fended off the blow with his staff, slanting it so that the axe did not bite. Again Jartan struck at him, and again Ivo parried, then struck in turn, checking the blow at the last moment so that the staff merely touched Jartan's neck.

"Well done," said Jartan, his craggy features relaxing. "I was afraid I might break your staff."

"So was I," said Ivo.

They had begun this game—which he knew Jartan did not consider a game—when Ivo was about eight or nine. Jartan had cut a staff for him, taught him to use it and told him that he must carry it with him at all times because he—Jartan—was going to try to take him unawares, and he must be prepared to protect himself. It had been difficult for him at first, for Jartan would strike at him suddenly with a stick or broom or a long-handled spoon, and Ivo would not always be able to ward off the blow. But now he no longer had to think about it, and it had been several years since Jartan had been able to touch him.

"What did you learn today?" asked Jartan.

"Nothing very much," said Ivo. "Yes, one thing. Neva asked if we would ever leave here, and Mistress Silvia said we would."

Jartan was examining the edge of the axe, running his thumb over it to see if it needed sharpening, and he paused.

"Did she say when?"

"When we wish to go for the right reason. Do you know what the right reason is, Jartan?"

"It's she who answers your questions, not I."

"But I'm sure you know."

"All I know is that I would not let you go for some time yet."

"Why not?"

"Because I don't think you're ready." He drove the axe into the log. "Get the swords."

"But you've been chopping wood most of the morning. Aren't you tired?"

"Get them!"

"Yes, Jartan."

He went into the hut and brought out the bucklers and blunt swords they used in their practise, and they faced one another in the center of the clearing. Usually at such times Jartan would do little attacking, only occasionally testing Ivo's defense. But on this day he not only attacked but pressed Ivo so hard that he was glad when Neva came back and he could stop.

Chapter 2

Several days later Ivo woke much earlier than usual without knowing why. He lay on his low wooden bed for a moment, listening. The sun was not yet up, and the forest was quiet except for the rustling stir of the leaves. Then he heard the sound that must have awakened him: a faint and far-off barking. Getting up, he put on his tunic and sandals, picked up his staff, and tiptoed out of his room. Jartan was still asleep in the alcove near the fireplace—he could hear his breathing—but as he opened the door of the hut Neva came out of her room and joined him.

"You heard it, too?" he asked.

"Yes. It came from over there."

They crossed the clearing and began running

towards the southern edge of the forest. There was no path here, but they knew the forest so well that in spite of that and the dim light they could move through it almost as quickly as one of the deer.

Reaching the edge of the forest, they paused and looked out over the heath. Some distance off, near the foot of a low hill, three large and shaggy dogs moved back and forth with their noses to the ground. Suddenly one of them picked up the scent that they had lost and, barking, came on again towards the forest with the other two following.

"They're tracking something," said Ivo. "I wonder what."

"Me," said a voice near them.

Turning, they saw Ronno sitting under a hawthorn. Two chickens lay on the ground near him.

"You've been raiding one of the farms again," said Neva.

"Yes."

"Why?"

"Lura will be having her cubs soon, and it's hard for her to hunt. So I have to do it for both of us."

"But you have the rest of the forest to hunt in," said Ivo.

"I know. And I did. But I've had bad luck for two days now."

The dogs were only a short distance away now, barking more and more excitedly. Though he knew there was no reason to be concerned, Ivo raised his staff. Then, when they were only a few feet from the edge of the forest, the dogs stopped, drawing back with the short hairs on the back of their necks bristling, not in anger, but in fear. They remained there for a moment, whining deep in their throats. There was a shrill, distant whistle, and looking up, Ivo and Neva saw a man standing on top of the hill. It was hard to see him clearly in that light and at that distance, but he seemed to be wearing a smock and carrying a spear. He came no nearer but whistled again and the dogs turned and ran back towards him, clearly happy to go.

Peering after them, Ivo moved forward until he was stopped by the invisible barrier that surrounded their part of the forest. But though it held him back, this time it seeemd to yield a little.

"You know," he said to Neva, "I think if I really tried, I could go out there."

"But you mustn't."

"Why not?"

"Because we're not supposed to." Then turning to Ronno, "You've got to be more careful. What would Lura do if you were caught?"

"There's not much chance of that," he said offhandedly.

"Well, you might be. If the hunting's been bad in the rest of the forest, isn't there any other place you could try?"

"There are some farms on the other side of the forest—to the north. But they're farther away."

"You're getting lazy," said Neva severely.

"No, I'm not. It's just harder to get there and back before dawn. But I think I'll keep away from that particular farm for a while." And picking up the chickens, he went off towards his den.

Jartan was up and baking oat cakes for their breakfast when they returned to the hut. He shook his head when they told him about Ronno.

"Why were the dogs afraid?" asked Ivo.

"Because of the spell that's been put on this part of the forest."

"Who put the spell on it? Mistress Silvia?"

"Yes."

"If they weren't afraid, could they have come in?" asked Neva.

"No. No one can come in who doesn't belong here."

"Is it possible that the spell isn't quite as strong as it was?" asked Ivo.

"Why do you ask?"

"Because the magic circle or whatever it is seemed to give a little when I pressed against it."

"I don't think it's gotten weaker. I think you've gotten stronger."

"Strong enough so that if I wanted to get out I could?"

"Why don't you ask Mistress Silvia that?"

"I will," said Ivo.

Jartan served the oat cakes and was thoughtful as they ate.

"Have you seen Greymane lately?" he asked finally.

"We see him almost every day," said Neva. "But we haven't had a riding lesson in some time."

"I think you should start having them again," said Jartan.

That was all he would say. But since, like Mistress Silvia, he never said anything without good reason, that afternoon they went to the large clearing where Greymane was grazing.

"Greetings, Greymane," said Ivo. "Jartan thought we should have some more riding lessons."

"Oh, he did?" said Greymane. "Well, I don't feel like it. It's too hot."

Ivo was about to argue with him when Neva caught his eye and shook her head. So he remained silent, and the two of them sat down at the edge of the clearing.

"What are you waiting for?" asked Greymane.

"We're not waiting for anything," said Neva. "We just thought we'd visit with you for a while."

"Don't try and fool me," said the grey charger. "You think if you stay here and talk politely to me I'll change my mind. But I won't."

"Very well," said Neva. "We'll try you again some other time." And she got up.

"Wait," said Greymane. "You both did fairly well

at your last lesson, but you still have a lot to learn. And if I don't teach you who will? So . . . All right, Neva. You first."

He came over to her and stood quietly while she mounted and then began circling the clearing, first walking, then trotting and finally cantering.

"Not bad," he said, stopping in the shade of a chestnut tree. "You have a good seat. Of course I don't know what your hands are like."

"Hands?"

"If you do any riding outside—and that must be why Jartan sent you here—it won't be like this. Your horse will have a saddle on him, and there'll be a bit in his mouth with reins to control him."

"What are they?" asked Ivo.

Greymane told them, and they both looked horrified.

"But that's awful!" said Neva. "Especially the bit. Why does anyone need them? Can't you just talk to the horse and tell him what you want him to do and where to go?"

"Horses can't talk outside the forest," said Greymane. "No animals can. At least people can't understand them."

"But why?"

"That's just the way it is. I was with Jartan for almost five years before we came here. But it was only after we got here that we were able to have a real conversation."

"If you can only talk to people outside, I'm not sure I'd like it there," said Neva.

"I don't think I would either," said Ivo. "And I still don't see why I'd need a saddle and reins."

"Oh, you don't? Do you think you could stay on my back if I didn't want you to?"

"I don't know why not."

"Let's see. Get down, Neva."

Neva slipped off his back, and Ivo mounted. Greymane started to trot across the clearing. Then suddenly he bucked, dropping his head and raising his hindquarters. Ivo went over his head and fell sprawling on the soft turf.

"Well?" said Greymane.

"You took me by surprise," said Ivo, getting to his feet. "Can we try it again?"

"If you like."

They tried it, not once but several times. And though each time it took him a little longer, in the end Greymane always did throw Ivo.

"I think that's enough for today," said the grey charger finally.

"I think so, too," said Ivo rubbing a sore shoulder.

"You were right about it's being too hot," said Neva looking at the sweat that darkened Greymane's coat. "We shouldn't have let you do it."

"Oh, I didn't mind. You're both good pupils. But from now on it might be better if we had the lessons early in the morning."

And so, for the next week or so, Neva and Ivo went to the clearing before they went to Mistress Silvia's cave. And by the end of that time even Greymane could find little fault with them as riders. It was about then that Lura had her cubs and Greymane went with Ivo and Neva to the den under the huge beech tree to congratulate Lura and Ronno.

Neva and Ivo were leaving the hut a few days later when they again heard dogs in the distance. However this time they sounded different for they were baying rather than barking. And as they stood there listening, Jartan came out of the hut and joined them.

"Those aren't farm dogs," he said. "They're hounds. Come on."

And he ran with them through the trees to the edge of the forest. When they reached it, the hounds, some six or eight of them, were just coming over the top of the hill. But this time there were three mounted men with them, riding behind them and urging them on. And their quarry, as they had all feared, was Ronno. He was at the foot of the hill, running hard for the safety of the forest.

"That fool fox!" said Greymane coming up behind them. "Didn't he know this might happen?"

"We warned him about it," said Neva. "But he's going to be all right, isn't he, Jartan?"

"I think so," said Jartan.

For Ronno was almost halfway to the forest and

holding the distance between himself and the hounds. But now a horn sounded off to the right, and a second pack of hounds and three more mounted men appeared, coming fast along the edge of the forest from a direction that would cut Ronno off.

Seeing them, Ronno checked and turned right also, but those watching knew that it was useless for, if he could not get to the forest, he was lost.

"Oh, no!" whispered Neva. "Isn't there anything we can do?"

"Greymane," said Ivo, "will you take me out there?"

"Get on," said Greymane.

"Ivo, don't!" said Neva. "You can't . . ."

But Ivo was on Greymane's back, leaning well forward and clutching his staff, and the charger was away, through the magic barrier and out on to the heath, thundering towards Ronno. Hard pressed though he was, Ronno sensed what they were going to do, and he swerved sharply to the left and raced towards the forest again. Greymane cut in behind him and, at a word from Ivo, stopped.

Ivo leaped off his back and, staff ready, waited for the oncoming hounds. Baying, jaws wide and eyes on Ronno, they paid no attention to Ivo. Stepping forward, he swung his staff low, sweeping the legs out from under the leader. With a startled yelp the hound went down and several of those that followed fell over him. The rest, further behind, circled wide away from Ivo, pausing as he ran towards them, shouting.

Then the hounds that had fallen struggled to their feet, and the pack went on again. But Ronno had been given all the time he needed. He and Greymane disappeared into the shelter of the trees while the hounds were still some distance away. When they reached the edge of the wood, Ivo saw them stop suddenly and draw back, whining, as the farm dogs had done, then he turned to face the riders who came galloping up behind them.

The first of these was a heavy-set man with a short black beard. Pulling his horse up, he glared down at Ivo.

"You knave!" he said. "How dare you interfere with a hunt?"

"I'm sorry," said Ivo. "I don't think I hurt any of your hounds, but . . ."

Before he could finish, the bearded man slashed down at him with his whip. Sliding his hands apart, Ivo raised his staff in a horizontal parry and the lash wrapped around it. But the knot at the tip flicked his cheek, drawing blood. Angered at this but even more at the man's manner, Ivo jerked down hard on the staff and pulled the man out of the saddle. He landed heavily and lay there for a moment, half stunned.

Now the other hounds and huntsmen reached them. One of these was a slim young man about Ivo's age. He wore a light green tunic with a silver belt.

"Are you hurt, Rendel?" he asked.

"No," said the bearded man, getting to his feet.

"No . . ." And drawing his sword he cut at Ivo.

Again Ivo threw up his staff and warded off the blow.

"Rendel, don't!" said the young man.

"I'll kill him!" said the bearded man, his face dark with rage, and he cut at Ivo a second and a third time. Though the blows came swiftly and savagely, they were so much slower than Jartan's that Ivo had no difficulty in parrying them. Then he struck in return, bringing his staff down on the man's hand and knocking his sword to the ground.

The man stepped back with a gasp, clutching his bruised knuckles.

"Seize him!" he ordered.

Leaping from their saddles, two of the huntsmen fell on Ivo, bearing him to the ground and holding him.

"That's enough, Rendel!" said the young man sharply.

"When he not only attacked the hounds but also attacked me?"

"Only after you had attacked him." He turned to Ivo. "Who are you?"

"Ivo."

"Where do you come from?"

"There," said Ivo, nodding towards the forest.

"He's lying!" said Rendel. "No one lives there. He comes from Brunn."

"Do you?" asked the young man.

"I don't even know where Brunn is."

"How can anyone not know that?" said Rendel. "I told you he's lying. He's a spy from Brunn, and we must take him back to Lantar with us."

"Must?" said the young man, frowning.

"The king will be very angry if we don't. He'll want to question him."

The young man looked at him and then at Ivo.

"Very well," he said. "Tie his hands."

One of the huntsmen took off his belt, tied Ivo's wrists with it and helped him to his feet.

"I'll take him," said the young man, holding out his hand.

"Yes, Your Highness," said the huntsman, and he gave him the end of the belt.

"Ride ahead," said the young man. "We'll follow."

Somewhat reluctantly, Rendel mounted. The huntsmen whistled to the hounds and they moved off slowly.

"Do you really live in the forest?" asked the young man.

"Yes," said Ivo.

"Why did you beat off the hounds?"

"I couldn't let them catch Ronno."

"Ronno?"

"The fox. I've known him since he was a cub."

"You're a strange young man. But also brave and skilful. Rendel is a very good swordsman. I never would have believed anyone could best him with a quarterstaff."

Ivo shrugged.

"I don't think you're from Brunn, and I think Rendel was wrong to attack you. If I let you go, could you get to the forest before the others got back here?"

Ivo measured the distance to the forest with his eye, then glanced at Rendel and the huntsmen. They were some distance ahead of them.

"Yes," he said.

"Hold up your hands, and I'll loosen the knot."

"What is your name?" asked Ivo as he did so.

"Liall."

"The huntsman called you Highness."

"The king is my uncle."

"Then you're a prince."

"Yes," said Liall. He glanced ahead. The hounds had picked up another scent, probably a rabbit, and Rendel and the other huntsmen were busy calling them off.

"Go," he said, pulling the belt from Ivo's wrists.

"Thanks," said Ivo. Then he was off, running for the forest. When he was thirty or forty yards from it, he heard shouts and looking back saw that Rendel and the huntsmen were galloping after him. Liall, much closer, had not moved. He was sitting on his horse, watching him. Ivo went on, reached the edge of the forest—and found he could not enter it!

The invisible barrier that had kept him in before

was now keeping him out. He hurled himself against it, but while it yielded he could not get through it. Then,

"Ivo, here!" said an urgent voice.

He turned. Neva was standing a few yards to his right. She was outside the line of trees, but one arm was still inside as if she were holding open a door. He ran to her. She took his hand and drew him inside. He glanced back. Liall was moving now. He had set his horse cantering towards the forest, and his eyes, fixed on the place where Neva had been standing, were wide with astonishment and admiration.

Chapter 3

"I still don't understand why Jartan wouldn't tell us," said Neva.

"Tell us what?" asked Ivo.

"Why the people of Andor hate Brunn so much."

"But he did. He said that they were at war. That they had been for years."

"But why? People don't fight with one another for no reason."

"Perhaps he didn't know."

"Of course he knows."

"Why do you say that?"

"I just think he does. He didn't say he didn't know. He just said we should ask Mistress Silvia."

"That's true."

It was the day after the incident with the huntsmen, and they were on their way to the cave. Ronno had been waiting just inside the forest with Jartan, and once Ivo was safe, had thanked him for what he had done. They had stood there for a while watching Liall and the others blundering around just outside the line of trees, trying to get into the forest and puzzled and angry because they couldn't. Then Neva and Ivo had gone to the cave and found that Mistress Silvia wasn't there. A squirrel who lived in one of the oak trees near the cave told them that Stekka the stag had hurt his leg and she had gone to tend him so they left. That evening they talked a good deal more about what had happened, and Jartan told them several things he had never told them before. For instance, they now knew that Brunn was the country that lay north of the forest and that the country to the south was called Andor.

"Then you agree that there's something strange about it?" asked Neva.

"I suppose so. Do you think Mistress Silvia knows what happened?"

"Of course she does." Then abruptly, "What color were his eyes?"

"Whose?"

"The prince's—Liall's."

"I'm not sure. I think they were brown."

"How can you not be sure?"

"Because I didn't really notice. All I was thinking

about was how I could get away."

"I don't know how you could have helped noticing. What color are mine?"

"What?"

"No," said Neva holding up her hand as he turned towards her. "Don't look."

"I don't have to look. They're green."

"Are you sure?"

"Of course I'm sure. They're dark green with gold lights in them."

"I don't know about the gold lights," said Neva, lowering her hand. "They are green. But you might have said they're pretty, too."

"Well, of course they're pretty," said Ivo. "They're very pretty. But you didn't ask me that. What's come over you anyway?"

"Nothing."

By this time they were crossing the glade, and looking up from her loom, Mistress Silvia smiled at them.

"Good morning, my lady," said Neva. "How is Stekka?"

"He'll limp for a few days, but then he should be as fleet as ever."

"He didn't break his leg, did he?" asked Ivo.

"No. He just wrenched it. I understand that while I was with him, you were busy, too."

"Oh. Yes."

"I am told that you did very well, Ivo."

"I couldn't let the hounds catch Ronno."

"No, of course not. And now you have questions

about what happened."

"Yes. Many questions. I imagine those men were hunting Ronno because he'd been raiding the farm."

She nodded. "The farmer must have told them about him. Though they would have hunted him anyway once the hounds picked up his scent."

"What would they have done if they had caught him? Eaten him?"

"No. They eat other game—deer, bears, wild boars—but not foxes."

"But then why were they hunting him?"

"Because they consider it sport."

"To hunt and kill when it's not even for food?"

"Yes."

"But that's awful!"

"Of course it's awful," said Neva. "But that's not the worst of it. One of them tried to kill Ivo!"

"I know."

"Why?"

"I gather because he was angry."

"Yes, he was. Ivo had pulled him from his horse. But to try and kill him . . . Are all men like that?"

"No. Not all."

"Just those from Andor then?"

"*Were* they all like that?"

"No," said Neva. "One of them—the prince, Liall—wasn't. He let Ivo escape."

"There are some in Brunn who would have done the same."

"It was because they thought I came from Brunn

that they wanted to take me with them," said Ivo. "Why do they hate one another so much?"

"It is a long story," said Mistress Silvia.

"Will you tell it to us?"

"I will tell you some of it. Once, many, many, years ago, Andor and Brunn were one kingdom ruled by a single king. Then came a day when the king, who had no children of his own, made the two sons of his sister his heirs, one to rule Andor, the southern part of the kingdom that lay between the forest and the mountains, and the other to rule Brunn, the northern part that lay between the forest and the sea. But neither was content with this. Both wanted to rule the whole kingdom, so they went to war and they and their children and their children's children have been at war ever since."

"And has no one done anything about it?" asked Neva. "Tried to make peace?"

"Yes. Lanis, the present king of Andor, approached Brennir, who at that time ruled Brunn, and for a while it looked as if there might be peace. But there was treachery; Brennir was killed; and ever since then, things have been worse then ever."

"What was the treachery?" asked Ivo.

Mistress Silvia did not answer. She was looking past him, and turning he saw that Jartan had entered the glade and was approaching the cave. This was strange enough for he never came there when Ivo and Neva were with Mistress Silvia. But that was not all. He was carrying a sword—not one of the blunt ones that he and Ivo practised with—but his own sword in the worn leather sheath that had always hung above his bed.

"Greetings, Jartan," said Mistress Silvia.

"My lady," he said, bowing.

She looked at him for a moment, then asked, "Where is he?"

"Close to where he was the other day. But he's riding west, towards the Burnt Place."

"Who is?" asked Ivo.

"Your friend, Prince Liall," said Jartan.

"But what is he doing here?"

"He seems to be looking for someone or something."

"For me?"

"Perhaps."

Ivo glanced at Neva. She had flushed slightly and dropped her eyes.

"Oh," he said. "I'd like to see him again. I never did thank him properly."

"I think you should go then," said Mistress Silvia. "You too, Neva."

"Yes, my lady," said Neva. And she, Ivo and Jartan moved off through the forest. They came to the edge near the place where Ivo had gone out, and there, as Jartan had said, was Liall. He was riding along slowly, studying the forest. Coming to a place where the trees were widely spaced, he turned and tried to ride in but his horse stopped and drew back. And when he tried to force the animal in, it reared and almost threw him.

Apparently this was not the first time it had happened for, though he looked disappointed, he did not seem surprised. Turning his horse left he rode on slowly, looking for another likely place to enter.

"Shall I call to him or go out there?" asked Ivo.

"No," said Jartan. "It's too late."

Looking south they saw half a dozen horsemen appear on top of the hill and come galloping towards the prince. He saw them at the same time, and though he frowned with annoyance, he waited for them. They were led by Rendel, the black-bearded man who had attacked Ivo, and they seemed to be a bodyguard rather than a hunting party, for this time they all wore byrnies and helmets and carried bucklers with a rampant bear on them. Rendel talked to the prince for several minutes, and he appeared to be remonstrating with him. But in the end they all went on together, riding west along the outside of the forest.

Neva, Ivo and Jartan followed them, moving silently and unseen behind the screen of trees and bushes. They had gone only a short way when Greymane joined them.

"What are you doing so far from your pasture?" Ivo asked him.

"Mistress Silvia sent me after you," he said.

"Why?"

"I don't know," he said.

Jartan did not seem surprised, so Ivo asked no further questions and they all went on together.

By now Liall and his guard had reached the Burnt Place, a circular open area several hundred yards across that was dotted with the charred stumps of trees. Nothing grew here; no shrubs, no grass, not even moss or lichen, and that may have been why Neva and Ivo had always found it disturbing and rarely came to this part of the forest. Though they had asked Mistress Silvia about it several times, all she would tell them was that it had been burnt many years before without saying how or why it seemed to be, not merely burnt, but blasted.

From the way the prince and the others looked about them, it was clear that they had never been there before, and it was just as clear that they did not like the place. But though Rendel talked to Liall even more emphatically and urgently than he had before, the prince dismounted and this time approached the forest on foot. He was just a few paces from it when there was a sudden thunder of hoofs and a score of men came galloping into the Burnt Place from the north. They, too wore helmets and byrnies, but their bucklers were blazoned with a sea serpent and their swords were in their hands.

"Quickly, Your Highness!" shouted Rendel and, drawing his sword, he spurred his horse forward between the prince and the oncoming riders. Liall turned and ran back towards him, but before he could mount the horsemen were on them.

"Who are they?" asked Ivo.

"Border guards from Brunn," said Jartan.

Swords were flashing and ringing now as the riders from Brunn attacked. Neva and Ivo watched in horror as men on both sides began falling. Though they knew that animals killed for food, until that moment, death had just been a word to them, an abstraction with only a tenuous connection with reality: the stoop of a falcon high in the blue, the distant cry of a rabbit in the night, a feather on Ronno's back. Now, suddenly, it was blood, white faces, unseeing eyes and awkwardly huddled bodies that would never move again.

Liall, still on foot, was trying desperately to defend himself. But he wore no mail and carried no buckler. One of the riders from Brunn cut down at him, and though he tried to parry, the blow beat down his guard and he staggered. Another blow, and he fell. Rendel, striking right and left, edged his horse closer to Liall, trying to protect him, but since Rendel was almost the last of the guard from Andor, it was apparent that he could not hold out much longer.

Staff in hand—the new staff he had cut to replace the one he had lost on the heath—Ivo started forward.

"Wait," said Greymane. "You can't go out there on foot."

"Nor with a staff," said Jartan. "Here." And he held out his sword.

"Ivo . . ." began Neva.

"He freed me," said Ivo, vaulting on to Greyman's back. "If I can save him, I must."

Then Greymane was away, bursting through the magic barrier and galloping towards the melee. Two of the riders from Brunn were attacking Rendel now. As one of them broke through Rendel's guard and he slid from his saddle, Greymane drove into the nearer of the two riders, and he and his horse went down. Leaping to the ground, Ivo picked up Liall, threw him across Greymane's back and mounted again. Recovering from his surprise, the second rider cut at Ivo. Ivo parried that stroke and another one, then Greymane had whirled and was racing back towards the forest.

As he had before, he burst through the magic barrier and stopped. Holding Liall in place with his left hand, Ivo looked back. Several of the riders from Brunn had started after him. But when their horses reached the edge of the forest, they reared, bucked and drew back as the huntsmen's steeds had done.

"Now what?" asked Ivo.

"Take him to the hut," said Jartan.

Chapter 4

"Put him there," said Jartan, nodding towards the alcove.

"Wouldn't my room be better?" asked Ivo. "We'll disturb him less there."

"Perhaps," said Jartan.

Neva opened the door for them, and they carried Liall in and lowered him onto Ivo's bed. His eyes were closed and his breathing was shallow and harsh. Jartan bent over him and examined his wounds: one on his forehead that did not seem deep or serious, and one on his chest that was still bleeding.

"Are they bad, Jartan?" asked Neva.

"This one is," said Jartan, studying the one on the chest.

"How bad?"

"Bad enough to be his death. Help me with his tunic, Ivo. And Neva, get some water."

Together Jartan and Ivo took off Liall's tunic, lifting and moving him gently. When Neva came back into the room with a basin of water, Mistress Silvia was with her.

"I'm glad you've come, my lady," said Jartan. "He needs your help."

"I thought he might," said Mistress Silvia.

She had a basket over her arm. Taking some dried, sweet-smelling herbs from it, she crumbled them into the water and washed the blood from the wounds, then examined them.

"Jartan said that one of them was bad," said Neva.

"Yes," said Mistress Silvia.

She took a small jar from the basket, dipped a finger in it and spread a green ointment on the wounds. Then she placed a hand on Liall's forehead and murmured something they could not hear. Almost at once his breathing became deeper, stronger. He stirred, opened his eyes and looked at her. He frowned slightly, puzzled. Then he saw Neva standing behind her and his face cleared. He smiled and closed his eyes again.

"He will sleep now," said Mistress Silvia. "You will tend him, Neva?"

"Yes."

"Then I will leave this with you." And she handed

over the basket with the herbs and ointment in it. "He should be well in two or three days. When he is, you may bring him to the cave."

"Yes, my lady."

With a last glance at the wounded prince, Mistress Silvia left the room. Jartan went with her.

"You know what to do?" asked Ivo.

"Of course."

"How do you know?"

"How do you think? It's one of the things she taught me."

Ivo watched as Neva took strips of the grey cloth Mistress Silvia wove from spider's silk and bound up Liall's wounds. Then, since it was apparent that she intended to stay there, he went out, closing the door behind him.

Jartan was sitting on the bench outside the hut. Mistress Silvia was gone.

"You did well when you went out to get him, Ivo," said Jartan. "Even better than when you saved Ronno. Were you afraid?"

"I didn't have time to be. Should I have been?"

"The riders from Brunn didn't know who you were. They probably thought you were from Andor, and they would have killed you if they could."

"I was too angry to think of that. Did they kill all the others?"

"All save one. He escaped."

"The one with the black beard—Rendel?"

"No. He is dead."

"I didn't like him, but he was brave. He did his best to protect Liall."

"He was the captain of his bodyguard. He was pledged to protect him even at the cost of his own life."

"Why did the riders from Brunn attack that way? Liall and those with him were doing nothing wrong."

"They were from Andor, and they were on or across the border."

"But to attack them . . . Not just attack but kill them! . . ."

"It is what happens when two countries hate and fear one another."

"Well, I'm glad that one of them escaped. He will tell the king that Liall is not dead."

"Let us say that the king will at least hope that Liall is not dead. And so he will do nothing—at least for the time being."

"What do you mean?"

"He will not know where Liall is. He may think that he was captured and he will send an emissary to Brunn to find out and offer ransom."

"By that time Liall will be well enough to leave here and go home."

"He may be," said Jartan. "In the meantime, since he has your room, we had better fix a place for you to sleep."

Taking the axe, they went off and cut pine boughs,

brought them back and piled them up next to the fireplace. They had just finished when Neva came out of Ivo's room.

"How is he?" asked Ivo.

"He seems better. He woke up a little while ago and wanted to know where he was and how he got here. I told him, and now he would like to talk to you."

"Are you coming in, too?"

"In a moment. He's thirsty and I'm going to brew some herb tea for him."

Ivo went in, and as Neva had said, Liall did look better than he had. He was no longer quite so pale and his eyes were clear.

"Neva told me what you did," he said simply but gravely. "I would like to thank you for it."

"There's no need to."

"When you saved my life?" He smiled faintly. "That would mean you don't value it at much."

"That's not so. I meant how could I do less after what you did for me?"

"I risked nothing by letting you go. You risked your life. I won't forget it. And neither will my uncle, the king." He hesitated a moment. "Did any of those with me escape?"

"Jartan says that one of them did."

"Then my uncle will know that I'm safe."

"He'll at least have reason to hope that you are." Now Ivo hesitated, then asked a question to which he was fairly sure he knew the answer. "Why did you come back here?"

"I was looking for you."

"But why?"

Liall shrugged. "Curiosity. There have been many stories about the forest. It has always been said that parts of it were enchanted, but it wasn't thought that anyone lived here. When I realized that what you had said was true—that this was where you came from —I thought I'd like to see you again."

"And also Neva."

"Yes," said Liall straightforwardly. "I only caught a glimpse of her but I was as curious about her as about you. When I leave here, I hope you'll both come back to Lantar with me."

"Lantar?"

"You know nothing about Andor?"

"Very little."

"Neva said neither of you had ever been outside the forest, but I found it hard to believe you had not heard of Lantar. It is our largest and fairest city."

Neva came back in now with a steaming goblet of herb tea and told Ivo that he'd better go, that after Liall drank it he should sleep again. Ivo left, thinking that she would be coming out shortly too, but she didn't. She remained with Liall for most of the afternoon and for a good part of the evening, too.

Though the bed of pine boughs was comfortable enough, Ivo did not sleep well that night, finding it strange to be there in the hut's big room rather than in his own. He lay awake for some time listening to the soft whispering of the trees, and when he did fall asleep his dreams were disturbing, for in them he was searching for something he had lost and he was not sure what it was.

When he woke in the morning, Jartan was already up, baking flat bread in the embers of the fireplace, and shortly after that Neva came out of her room and went in to see how Liall was. He had slept very well, she reported later, and was feeling much stronger, but he would still need care and so she thought she would stay with him rather than go to the cave with Ivo.

At first Ivo thought he would not go either. But when he discovered that Jartan was going to be working in the garden, he changed his mind and set off alone.

Mistress Silvia was at her loom and she nodded when he greeted her.

"Where is Neva?" she asked.

"With Liall."

"How is he?"

"Better. But she thought she should stay with him."

"He will be even better this afternoon. He should get up then and perhaps tomorrow he can come here with you."

"I'll tell that to Neva."

"Do you have any questions for me?"

"Yes. When will he be able to leave here?"

"He will be able to leave the day after tomorrow. But he may not wish to leave then."

"Why not? He knows that his uncle, the king, is concerned about him."

"He might decide that it won't really matter if he stays for a few more days. Don't you want him to stay?"

"Of course. I like him. I asked because he said that when he did leave he wanted Neva and me to go with him."

"And do you want to go?"

"I don't know. I told you I'd like to see other places and other people sometime. But I never thought of going with someone else."

"You mean you thought you'd go just with Neva."

"Yes."

"Do you have any other questions?"

"Let me think." He frowned, feeling guilty because he did not have any important ones ready. "Why couldn't I get back into the forest the other day when I went out to help Ronno?"

"I'm sure you know."

"Because of the spell you put on this part of it. But Ronno had no trouble getting in or out. And Greymane didn't seem to have either."

"No. But the spell works differently in almost every case. I knew the animals who belonged here would want to be able to leave and come back. And when I first cast it, its purpose was as much to keep you in as to keep others out."

"I'm not sure I understand."

"Don't try to. It's magic, and it has its own laws. What else?"

"I don't think I have any more questions."

"No?"

"Why are you smiling?"

"Because I know there are other things on your mind and I was wondering whether you'd talk about them."

"What things?"

"Haven't you been upset because Neva has been spending so much time with Liall?"

"Why should I be? She's only doing it because he was wounded and needs care. Besides, I told you I liked him."

"Yes."

He frowned again, aware that—as always—there were things she was trying to get him to see.

"All right. Why is she doing it?"

"You just told me why."

"I know. But there's more to it than that, isn't there? I'm Ivo whom she's known all her life and he's someone new who can talk to her about things that I can't: about Andor and the palace at Lantar and what it's like to be a prince."

"And is that all they talk about—things?"

"What else is there to talk about?"

"Why don't you ask Neva?" said Mistress Silvia, smiling again.

"Because I don't care." He got up abruptly. "I think I'll go, my lady."

"Very well. And if Liall comes here with you tomorrow, tell Jartan to come too."

"Yes, my lady," he said and left, thinking about what she'd said and also about the rather strange feelings that he had apparently had for some time but that he had not been conscious of till he talked to her.

He didn't go directly to the hut but stopped by the pond first and watched the otters at play, then went to the large clearing to visit Greymane. When he finally returned to the hut, Jartan had finished working in the garden and told him to get the swords and bucklers for some weapon practise.

They had only been at it for a short time when Jartan paused and said, "What's wrong with you today?"

"Why?"

"I've touched you three times now. You're not thinking about what you're doing—not that you should have to think. If you want to stop, say so."

"I'm sorry, Jartan. No, let's not stop. Let's try it again."

While they were talking, Neva came out of the hut and sat down on the bench. Liall was sleeping again, she told them, and she agreed that he seemed strong enough to get up when he woke. She had a needle and thread with her and was mending something. As she held it up, Ivo saw that it was Liall's tunic. She had washed the blood from it and was now sewing up the place where he had been wounded.

"Well, Ivo?" said Jartan.

Ivo raised his buckler and instead of waiting for Jartan to attack him, he attacked himself—so vigorously that Jartan gave back before him. When they finally stopped, Jartan nodded approvingly but asked why he seemed to be in such a temper.

Liall did get up that afternoon, sat out in the sun and remained up so that, for the first time, they all had supper together. He began asking Jartan questions, wanting to know if he had always lived in the forest and, if not, where he had come from. But when Jartan made it clear that he did not want to talk about it, Liall dropped the subject and again began urging Neva and Ivo to come back to Lantar with him when he left.

Though Liall seemed himself again, he began to look tired during supper and went to bed soon after it. Ivo, however, was restless and went out, walking to the edge of the forest where he stood for a while, looking out over the moonlit heath. When he came back, Neva was again sitting on the bench outside the hut.

"I've seen little of you all day," she said.

"I know."

"What did Mistress Silvia have to say this morning?"

"That if Liall was well enough to come to the cave tomorrow, Jartan should come, too."

"Oh."

"You don't seem surprised."

"No. If we're going to be leaving here, she will have things to say to us and she will want Jartan to hear them also."

"Are we going to be leaving here?"

"Yes, of course."

"Why of course."

"It's just a feeling I have."

"And where will we be going? To Lantar with Liall?"

"Perhaps. Perhaps not. Don't you want to go?"

"I don't know."

"I thought you did. You always said you did."

"I know. And while I'd like to see other places, I always hoped that when we went it would be for something more than that."

"It will be."

"Why do you say that?"

"Don't you remember what Mistress Silvia said when we asked her about it? 'You will go when you wish to go for the right reason.' "

"And what is the right reason?"

"We'll probably find out tomorrow. Did she have anything else to say?"

"She wanted to know if I was upset because you were spending so much time with Liall."

"And are you?"

"No. I told her I knew you were doing it because you had to take care of him."

"I didn't *have* to. Jartan could have done it just as well as I."

"Then why have you been doing it?"

"Why do you think?"

"Because you wanted to. Because you like being with him."

"That's right. You should go see Mistress Silvia without me more often." Though it was too dark to see her face, he knew she was smiling just as Mistress Silvia had.

"This is silly," he said, annoyed. "We've never talked about anything as silly as this before."

"No, we haven't," said Neva, getting up. "Good night." And she went into the hut.

Chapter 5

As Mistress Silvia had predicted, the next morning Liall said that he felt as well as he ever had. So after breaking their fast together, they all set out for the cave: Neva, Ivo, Liall and Jartan.

It was another fine day. What they could see of the sky was clear and blue; a faint breeze rustled the leaves, and the trees were alive with birds that twittered, sang and darted from branch to branch overhead.

"It's very beautiful here," said Liall, looking around admiringly. "Quite different from the parts of the forest I've been in to the east."

"Different how?" asked Ivo.

"Though the trees are not as tall there, the forest

seems much darker and less friendly."

"What were you doing when you went there?" asked Jartan.

"Hunting," said Liall. "Sometimes deer, but mostly wild boar."

"Then why should the forest have been friendly?"

"I don't understand."

"There is no hunting, no killing of any sort here, either by us or by any of the animals who live here."

"But why?"

"Because that is the law. Those animals that must kill to live do it elsewhere."

They were almost at the pond now, walking in single file. Suddenly Ronno came trotting down the path and paused when he saw them.

"Good morning," he said to Neva who was leading the way. Then looking at Liall, who was immediately behind her, "I see that your friend is better."

"Yes, he is," she said.

"I'm glad," said Ronno. "I know you were worried about him. But why is he staring at me that way?"

"I don't know," said Neva. "Why are you, Liall?"

"Because, unless I'm still feverish, he's talking."

"Oh. I'd forgotten what Greymane told us: that the animals outside can't talk. Or at least that people can't understand them."

"No, they can't," said Liall. "Is this Ronno?"

"Yes. Why?"

"If it is, I'd like to ask his pardon."

"If it's for what happened the other day," said Ronno, "I'll admit that I was frightened. I don't mind a good run. But when that second pack of hounds appeared, I thought I was done for. And of course I would have been if it hadn't been for Ivo."

"I can say the same thing," said Liall.

"So I hear. Remember how you felt then, when you thought you were finished, the next time you go hunting."

"I will. Though I'm beginning to doubt if I shall do it anymore."

"You needn't go that far," said Ronno with a grin. "I do a little hunting myself. But why hunt foxes? We're not good to eat."

"Very well," said Liall. "I'll promise you that much. No matter what I do, I'll never hunt a fox again."

"That more than makes amends for the day we met," said Ronno, and he went trotting off towards his den.

"I understand now why you wanted to save him, Ivo," said Liall. "Just as I'm beginning to understand many other things."

Mistress Silvia was outside her cave, and two of the spiders were with her, clinging to the rocks overhead and spinning out thread that she wound on a spindle. She looked up as the four of them approached, cut the threads and the spiders disappeared into the cave.

"So the report Ivo gave me yesterday was true,"

she said to Liall. "I thought you would be well enough to come here today, and I'm glad you are."

"I have you to thank for that, my lady," he said, making her a deep reverence.

"Not I alone."

"No. And I have already thanked Ivo and Neva for what they did for me. But it is you I must thank most of all. For I know how grievously I was hurt, and I do not believe I would be here now if it were not for your help."

"That could well be."

"Was it leechcraft that saved me or magic?"

"Does it matter?"

"No. What matters is that you did give me back my life. And what I would like to know is how I can repay you."

"You have already said that what was done was not done by me alone. How do you intend to repay Ivo and Neva?"

"I'm not sure. We haven't talked about it. But I've asked them both to come back to Lantar with me when I leave here. My uncle, the king, will be as grateful to them, as I am."

"Are you suggesting that I come, too?"

She was smiling now, a faint grave smile. Liall shook his head.

"No, my lady."

"Why not?"

"Because, while I would like you to come—and the

king would like it, too—I don't think you would come. Nor do I know why you should."

"Why do you say that?"

"Because, as I told Ivo a short while ago, I understand many things now that I did not understand before. This is your realm, a place like no other that I have ever heard of, where men and animals live together in friendship. Why should you leave it—this place where there is no killing—and go out into a world that is full of war and hatred?"

She looked at him thoughtfully.

"You do not like what is happening there?"

"No, my lady. Though my father was killed in a battle not far from here, and though, but for your help, I would have been killed, too, I do not hate those from Brunn. In fact, I have always hoped that some way could be found to end our differences so that there could be peace between us."

Ivo, who had been listening intently, stirred.

"Is there some way that can be done, my lady?"

"There may be."

"How?"

"I cannot tell you that, but I can tell you how you can find out. The answer was written long ago on a stone set on the top of Tarec."

"On Tarec?" said Liall. "It might as well be on the moon."

"Why so?" asked Ivo. "What is this Tarec?"

"It is the highest peak of the Wendery Hills that

lie between Andor and Brunn, far to the west beyond the Desert of Morven. But none may climb it."

"It is that great a mountain?" said Ivo. "That difficult to climb?"

"Not as great or difficult as many of those to the south. But it is a sacred mountain. For it was there that Kennar, our ancestor, had his first sight of Andor; and where he stood, no man may set his foot."

"It is forbidden?" asked Neva.

"There is no need for that. Of those who have tried to climb Tarec, few have come back and those few had lost their wits. It is said that there is something there—a watcher—to keep all from it." He paused. "Of course, there are many tales told about this part of the forest, too, and yet I am here."

"You are thinking that you will go there then?" asked Ivo.

"If the stone will tell me what I want to know, perhaps I should."

"I must warn you that the stone is now broken," said Mistress Silvia. "But it may be that what was written on it can still be read."

"If I take the risks of the journey there, I will risk that too." He hesitated a moment. "Very well. I will go."

"Good," said Ivo. "I will go with you."

"*We* will go with you," said Neva.

"We?" Liall stared at her. "Do you doubt what I said about Tarec?"

"No."

"Then be reasonable. Even to reach it will be a great trial, for we will have to cross Morven, which is a desolate waste."

"I am still going."

Liall looked at Ivo and then at Mistress Silvia.

"My lady, what say you to this?"

"Ivo has wanted to leave here for some time, and Neva has said that when he left she wanted to go with him. Some days ago I told them that they could both leave when they wished to leave for the right reason. There can be no better reason than this."

"I still think it will be a very dangerous and difficult journey," said Liall. "But if you do not . . ."

"I did not say it would not be," said Mistress Silvia. "I said that if she wished to go, she should be permitted to."

"Very well," said Liall. "All that remains then is to decide when we can leave."

"I think," said Jartan, "that this is why you wanted me here, my lady."

"Yes, Jartan."

"There are preparations that must be made. But I have already started them, and if all three of them help, I think that they can leave tomorrow morning."

"There are things that I must do, too," said Mistress Silvia. "Tomorrow then."

"We will see you again before we go?" asked Neva.

"Would you go without that?"

"No, my lady," said Neva.

They started across the glade and along the path to the hut. Ivo was walking slowly, lagging behind, and glancing at him, Neva said, "You seem troubled, Ivo. Do you think, as Liall does, that I should not be coming with you?"

"No. I'm sure it will not be easy, but if it were too dangerous I don't believe Mistress Silvia would let you go."

"She might, if what we were trying to do were important enough."

"There's little doubt that it's important. But that's made me wonder. It was many days ago that she said we could leave when we wished to for the right reason. Do you think she knew then that we would be leaving and why?"

"Of course."

"Even though that was before we'd ever seen Liall?"

"Yes."

"I think she did, too—that she knew he would be coming. And that makes me wonder about something else. Jartan said he had already started making preparations for our journey. Well, isn't it possible that many of the things we have been doing and learning recently were part of those preparations?"

She smiled at him. "Dear Ivo. It sometimes takes you a while to see things, but in the end you usually do."

"You mean you think that, too?"

"I've thought so for a long time."

"How long?"

"Several years."

"That we were being prepared for something . . . No, not something. For this particular quest?"

"Yes."

"Why didn't you tell me?"

"I thought that when the time came you would find out."

"But if that's true, then what we're going to do—try to do—could well be part of something else. Something even larger."

"Yes."

"Do you know what it is?"

"No. But again I think that in time we may find out."

They had reached the hut now, and though Ivo had many more questions, he did not have a chance to ask them for there was too much to do to prepare for the journey. One of the things that Jartan had done was to weave three flat baskets out of osiers and fix them with slings so they could carry them on their backs. While he and Neva began baking faring-bread—flat cakes that would keep for some time—he had Ivo and Liall hollow out gourds to use as water bottles. For, he told them, they would find no food or water in the desert.

Though Liall knew of the Wendery Hills, he had

never been there so that evening Jartan drew a map on a piece of bark showing them the route across Morven and the approach to Tarec. It would, he thought, take them about three days to cross the desert. They should travel early in the morning and late in the afternoon, resting during the middle of the day when the sun was hottest. And they should, if they could, avoid the Hiltis, the wandering people who lived in the desert and were hostile, not only to strangers, but to one another.

The next morning they filled the water bottles and packed the baskets with faring-bread, which they had wrapped in leaves. They also put in some of the dried fruit that remained from their winter store.

"You will need more of a weapon than that," said Jartan as Ivo picked up his staff. "Here." And taking his sword from the pegs on which it rested over his bed, he held it out.

"Your own sword?"

"You used it well the other day, and I know you will not use it again unless you must. It's mine no longer. It's yours."

"Thank you, Jartan," said Ivo, touched, and he buckled it on.

"I have one for you, too, Liall," said Jartan. "It may not be the equal of the one you lost in the battle, but it is a serviceable blade." And he gave him one of the practise swords, which he had sharpened. Liall thanked him also, slipped it into his sheath, and they set out for the cave.

Mistress Silvia was waiting for them, and she was not alone. Greymane was with her and Ronno and Lura and their cubs and Dahga and Sim and Stekka the stag. In fact, most of their friends were there, gathered in a great circle around the entrance to the cave.

"Stop that," said Ronno to his cubs, who had been playing with Sim and now ran clumsily towards Ivo and Neva, barking a greeting. And as they became quiet and came back to him, "We heard that you were leaving and wanted to say goodbye to you."

"You'll be coming back, won't you?" asked Sim.

"Of course we will," said Neva. "Good morning, my lady."

"Good morning," said Mistress Silvia. "I take it that you're ready to go."

"Yes, my lady," said Ivo.

"I have some things for you. This is for you, Neva." And she gave her a packet of dried herbs. "And these are for all of you." And she gave them each a travelling cloak woven of spider's silk. They thanked her and folding them small, packed them in their baskets.

"Jartan has told you how you should go?"

"Yes, my lady."

"There are things he could not tell you—dangers that you will face. But," and she looked at Ivo and Neva, "you two at least are as prepared for them as you can be."

"I know, my lady," said Neva.

"Yes. You have known it for some time. But what you do not know is how much hangs on what you are trying to do."

"We have guessed that it is important," said Ivo.

"It is more than important. And not for just Andor and Brunn. More than that I will not say lest, instead of giving you strength, it make you anxious. But wherever you go and whatever happens, my thoughts and my love will go with you."

"And our thoughts will be with you, my lady," said Neva. "With all of you."

"No, child. They will not. For when you leave here, you will forget everything you do not need to know for your quest."

"We will not forget you," said Neva. "We could not!"

"You will—until you see me again."

"But we will see you again, will we not?"

"If your quest is successful. If it is not, then that will be only a small part of the loss we all will suffer. And now come here."

Neva went to her, and she looked into Neva's eyes for a moment, gravely and tenderly, and then embraced and kissed her and did the same to Ivo.

"Fare you well," she said. "And you, too, Liall."

"My lady," he said. She held out her hand to him, and he dropped to one knee and pressed his lips to it.

"I will go with you to the edge of the forest," said Jartan and set off across the glade. They followed him, pausing when they reached the far side and looking back. Mistress Silvia had not moved. She sat there, beautiful and regal, surrounded by all the creatures, great and small, of the forest. Then they went on again.

Jartan led the way through the trees, past oak, ash and pine, until they came to a stand of birches that bordered the heath. He looked at Neva and Ivo as Mistress Silvia had done, his craggy face softer than they had ever seen it. Then, without a word, he embraced them and forcing open the magic barrier, stood aside as they and Liall went past him out of the shelter of the forest.

THE QUEST

Chapter 6

It was pleasant out on the heath. The sun was behind them and the turf was firm but yielding underfoot. They were walking due west, Ivo between Neva and Liall.

Ivo took a deep breath, enjoying the clean scent of the forest pines that the breeze brought to them, and glanced at Liall who smiled at him. Then he looked at Neva. Her stride was just as long and easy as Liall's, but she was frowning slightly.

"Is your basket too heavy for you?" he asked.

She raised the pack basket a little higher on her back but shook her head.

"Then what is it?"

"Nothing," she said.

Ivo did not press her. When she was ready to tell him what was wrong, she would. He looked ahead. The forest came to an end a long bowshot ahead of them. At least there was a break in it, and the trees on the far side seemed to grow less thickly. In the open space, something dark moved; something quite large or they would not be able to see it at that distance. As Ivo looked at it, wondering what it was, a faint uneasiness came over him; a foreshadowing of something disturbing that he could not identify anymore than he could the dark, shifting shape in the center of the open space.

Neva and Liall were looking ahead also, clearly as puzzled as he was. They went on and, seeing the charred tree stumps, realized that the reason the area was open was that this part of the forest had been burnt down. At the same time the dark mass broke apart and resolved itself into a dozen or more vultures and carrion crows that rose heavily into the air and went flying off with hoarse cries.

They were at the edge of the Burnt Place now, and near its centre where the birds had gathered were the skeletons of three horses, all that remained of their ghoulish feast. A little to the left, out on the heath, were five grave mounds, each with a sword thrust into it to identify it. Liall walked over to one of them, his face sober.

"This is Rendel's," he said.

Neva and Ivo said nothing.

"It is on our side of the border," he went on, "and besides the riders from Brunn would not have buried them. That means that my uncle sent men here to look for my body and must know now that I am still alive."

"Yes," said Ivo. And after a moment, "There's nothing that can be done here. Let's go on."

Liall nodded, and they set off again, continuing westward. Liall was frowning now, too, and finally he said, "I know that I was wounded, Ivo. That you rescued me, and Neva took care of me afterwards. But I can't remember anything else: how you saved me or where you took me after that."

Though the sun was warm, Ivo suddenly felt chilled and a little ill. He knew now what had been disturbing him, why he had felt uneasy.

"I can't remember either," he said.

Liall stopped and stared at him.

"You can't?"

"No."

"That's impossible! I was hurt and was probably unconscious for a while, but you weren't. How could you not remember?"

"I don't know, but I can't. Can you, Neva?"

"No," she said.

"Was that why you were looking upset before?"

"Yes. It suddenly came over me that while I knew who I was and who you and Liall were, I didn't know anything else."

"Nothing?"

"Oh, I know where we're going and why: to try and find the stone on the top of Tarec and see if we can bring peace to Andor and Brunn. But that's all. I don't know how I know that or where we lived before we started on this journey."

"Nor do I," said Ivo. "I can't remember anything before the moment when I asked you if your basket was too heavy for you."

"You mean you can't remember your childhood, who your parents are or where you lived?" asked Liall.

"No," said Ivo. "Can you?"

"Of course. I remember everything until a short while ago when I was out hunting with Rendel. A farmer told us about a fox that had been raiding his chickens and we went after him." He paused. "Then there's a blank. I came back here looking for someone or something, and Rendel and my guard followed me and that's when we were attacked."

"You're not so badly off as we are then," said Ivo. "You can't have lost more than a few days, but Neva and I have lost everything—all the years we've lived. And it's frightening."

"It's more than frightening," said Neva, her voice unsteady. "It's not just the years that have been lost. I feel lost, too. For when you don't know who you were, you don't know who you are."

"But you do know who you are," said Liall. "You're Neva and Ivo."

"What does that mean?" said Ivo. "They're merely names. The first question you asked us was, 'Can't you remember your parents or where you lived?' And we can't. That's all gone."

"Not forever. I'm sure it will come back to you."

"When?"

"It depends on why you can't remember. And I think it's because a spell was put on you."

"A spell?"

"Yes. Parts of the forest are said to be enchanted. You may have wandered into it and been ensorcelled."

"But then you must have been too. And if so why have you only forgotten a few things while we have forgotten everything?"

"I don't know. But something else occurs to me. I have a feeling that whatever happened to us has something to do with the stone."

"Why do you say that?"

"Because it is the one thing we all remember. And if that is so, then isn't it possible that when we find it, the spell will be lifted?"

"I suppose it's possible," said Ivo. "What do you think, Neva?"

She shrugged. "Who can tell? In any case, we have little choice. We can't go back because we don't know where to go, so we might as well go on."

"To Tarec?"

"Where else?"

"Very well." The look on her face wrung his heart,

and he moved towards her. "Neva . . ."

"Don't!" she said sharply. "There's nothing you can say that will help." And she started forward again. Ivo and Liall exchanged glances.

"I'm sorry," said Liall. "I know how deeply disturbing it must be. And still I'm sure that in time you will remember. After all, you're not alone. Though it's gone at the moment, you and your sister both share the same past, have the same memories, and . . ."

"Sister?"

"Well, Neva is your sister, isn't she?"

"I don't know," said Ivo slowly. "I suppose . . . Yes, she must be."

They went on after her. And though they walked quickly and soon left the Burnt Place far behind them, the sense of desolation that had come over Ivo there remained with him. Lost, Neva had said. That was how he felt too. Lost, suddenly cut off from everything he had been. And along with that sense of loss, there was something else—an additional feeling of deprivation that was all the more disturbing because he could not identify it.

The forest to their right began to thin out, the trees becoming more spindly and growing farther apart, and the grass of the heath became drier and the bare places more frequent. Then all at once, they were at the end of the heath and Morven was before them. It stretched out ahead of them and to the right and left as far as they could see, a waste of white sand without a tree or blade of grass anywhere.

They paused there for a moment, studying it, and Ivo forced himself to think of what he did remember instead of what he didn't.

"As I recall, we're to go due west, and it should take us three days to cross." Neva and Liall nodded. "We have three water gourds. I suggest that we use one each day and that sparingly."

Again Neva and Ivo nodded, and adjusting their pack baskets, they went forward. There would be no difficulty about keeping their direction. Since the morning sun was still low, their shadows pointed the way for them. But the walking here was much harder than it had been on the heath, for the sand was soft and they sank into it almost to their ankles. As they plodded on, climbing any low dunes that they encountered and going around the ones that were too tall, Ivo found himself wondering how they all knew that it would take them three days to cross the desert. Clearly they had been told so, but by whom? Again and again he tried to think back, recall a face or a place, but he could remember nothing before that moment on the heath when he first began to sense that something was wrong.

On they went following their shadows, their eyes narrowed against the glare of the sun on the white sand. But as the sun rose higher, their shadows became smaller until, when it was directly overhead, they disappeared.

"I think we should rest now," said Neva, pausing in a hollow between two dunes. "We were told we should in the middle of the day."

"Here?" asked Liall.

"It's as good a place as any," said Ivo. "There's no shade anywhere."

"No," said Neva. "But there are our capes."

As soon as Neva mentioned them, Ivo recalled them also. Unslinging their baskets, they took out the capes. They were silvery grey and very light but seemed to be strong. When they put them on, they found that they had hoods, which they raised to protect their heads from the sun, and, thus shielded, they were more comfortable than they had been since they had left the heath.

They found dried fruit and flat cakes wrapped in green leaves in their baskets and they ate a little of each. But though they were not very hungry, they were thirsty. None of them had touched their water gourds since they had entered the desert, and they decided that on this first day they would use Ivo's. He took it from his belt, unstoppered it and gave it to Neva. They each drank and then stretched out with their backs against the dune and rested.

Ivo had closed his eyes to rest them after the glaring of the sun and he must have fallen asleep for when he opened them the sun was no longer overhead. He woke Neva and Liall, and they went on again, this time walking towards the sinking sun.

They trudged on all afternoon, going steadily westward. They kept their capes on, the hoods raised, and found that this did much to make the heat bearable. When the sun began to set, they stopped again beside a large dune, ate and finished the water in Ivo's gourd.

They sat there, watching the sun go down and the stars appear. They were very bright and in the clear air of the desert they seemed to be very close. Once the sun was gone, it began to get cold; but they discovered that though the cloaks were light in weight they were warm. The three wondered, as they had before, what the cloaks were made of and where they had come from.

Ivo lay there for some time, looking at the stars and thinking about many things, but mostly about Neva. He had watched her through most of the day, concerned lest their desert crossing prove too much for her. But she had kept their pace with no difficulty, and when they stopped she seemed less tired than Liall.

Liall was asleep now, but Neva, lying next to Ivo, did not seem to be for he heard her stir.

"Can't you sleep either?" he whispered.

"No."

"What are you thinking about?"

"Probably what you are."

"All the things we don't know."

"Yes."

"Do you think, as Liall does, that a spell was put on us?"

"It seems likely. How else could we have forgotten

everything but what we're to do?"

"But who could have put it on us? And why?"

"If we knew the one, we'd probably know the other. But while it may make things difficult for us, I don't think it was an evil spell. At least I don't think whoever put it on us is evil."

"Neither do I. There's one other thing."

"Yes?"

"Liall seems to think we're brother and sister. Do you?"

It took her so long to answer that he was afraid she wasn't going to. But finally,

"Yes," she said. "I do."

"Why?"

"Because we've both forgotten the same things, much more than Liall has. But more important, while I like Liall, I don't feel I know him very well. But I do feel I know you, everything about you. That we've always been together."

"Yes," said Ivo. "I feel that way, too."

He settled back, trying again to catch a glimpse of what lay behind the curtain that cut them off from the past, but he could remember nothing. All he had was this day and the sense that he and Neva were very close. And as he thought about all the things that seemed familiar to him—the way she moved and frowned and talked—he fell asleep.

The sky was just becoming pink when they woke the next morning. They ate and drank some water, and as soon as the sun was high enough to give them their direction they set off again westward. About mid-morning the dunes became smaller and fewer and finally disappeared. With no need to climb them or go around them, they were able to travel faster, walking steadily towards the line, wavering in the heat, where the endless stretch of white sand seemed to meet the sky.

When the sun was directly overhead and they were about to rest, they saw some tall, dark shapes in the distance. They looked as if they might be trees so they went towards them. But when they reached them, they saw that they were a strange kind of desert plant. They were greenish grey, taller than a man and almost as thick as a man's body with a few upward thrusting limbs, and they bristled with fine thorns.

Liall said that though he had never seen them before he had heard about them. They were called *doranc*, and they were only found here in the Morven.

Though the *doranc* had no leaves and gave no shade, they were alive, the first living things they had seen since they entered the desert, and so the three sat down nearby for their midday meal. None of them was hungry and they ate as little as they had when they had broken their fast; but they were all thirsty and had to restrain themselves when Neva passed round her water gourd; Liall confessing that he could empty it by himself.

Wrapping themselves in their cloaks, they rested and dozed until midafternoon, then went on again. They continued westward for some time, keeping their hoods well forward to protect their eyes from the sun's glare. Shortly before sunset the flat whiteness of the desert was broken by a low range of weathered rocks. At the same time, high above them in the cloudless blue sky they saw two large birds wheeling and circling.

"Vultures," said Neva.

Ivo nodded. Though none of them said any more, they all knew that the carrion birds were watching something, something on which they thought or hoped they could feast as they had on the dead horses in the Burnt Place. Was it the three of them?

They trudged on towards the rocks. When they were little more than a bowshot from the nearest one, they saw something moving, something white. It came towards them unsteadily, uncertainly. Then, apparently seeing them, it turned away, stumbled a few hasty steps and collapsed on the sand.

"It's not an animal," said Ivo. "It must be a Hilti."

"We were told to avoid them," said Liall.

Without knowing how, Ivo knew this, too.

"But this one is hurt or ill," said Neva, and she went towards the white shape, Ivo and Liall following her. When they reached it, they saw that it was a figure in a long white robe, its head swathed in a white turban, lying face down in the sand. Ivo and

Liall kneeled, turned the figure over, and raised its head. Though the turban covered its face as well as its head, leaving only the eyes exposed, somehow they knew that it was not a man but a woman; an old woman.

Her eyes were closed, but as they raised her head the lids fluttered up and she looked at them, first blankly, then with terror.

"Don't be afraid," said Liall. "Tell us what's wrong."

She did not answer but only stared at them with eyes that were filled with fear. Kneeling also, Neva pulled down the cloth that covered the old woman's face and saw that it was thin and drawn and that her lips were so dry that they had cracked.

"She's starving," said Neva. "But she needs water more than anything else." And she took the gourd from her belt and and removed the stopper.

"Wait," said Ivo. "You know that we've only what's left in your gourd and Liall's to see us across Morven."

"Of course I know," said Neva. "But we can't let her die, can we?"

"No," said Ivo. "Of course not."

Neva put the gourd to the old woman's lips. Her hands went up, clutching it, and she began drinking greedily. Ivo watched, hoping she would stop, but she only lowered it when the gourd was empty and then looked hopefully at Ivo's and Liall's.

"Mine's empty, too," said Ivo. "All we have left is

his," nodding towards Liall's, "and we need that."

"Perhaps we can let you have some more later," said Neva. "Carry her over there, and we'll give her something to eat."

Ivo picked her up—she weighed no more than a child—carried her to the foot of the nearest rock and put her down in its shadow. Neva took some of the flat faring-bread from her basket and offered it. The woman took it and began eating it, but not as eagerly as she had taken the water.

"Are you lost?" asked Liall.

The old woman shook her head.

"Where are your people?"

The old woman pointed behind her, to the west.

"Then why aren't you with them? Why are you wandering around here by yourself?"

The old woman gestured.

"They chased you away?"

The old woman nodded.

"But why?" asked Neva.

"I've heard," said Liall, "that the Hiltis are hostile to everyone, even one another. They probably sent her away to die."

"Is that true?" asked Neva.

Again the old woman nodded.

"Well, we won't let you die," said Neva. "We'll share what we have with you."

The old woman looked at her uncomprehendingly, then her eyes became veiled.

"It's getting late," said Ivo, "and I don't think she's strong enough to travel any farther. We'd better camp here tonight."

Neva and Liall agreed, and they sat down next to the old woman. Though they knew they had to save their water, they had had none since noon and they were so parched that they could not eat until they had each taken a small swallow from Liall's gourd. He gave some more to the old woman, then tied it to his belt again.

The old woman lay back against the rock and closed her eyes.

"What kind of people drive their old away to die?" asked Neva.

"The Hiltis, for one," said Liall.

"But why?"

"Because she *is* old, and it's probably not easy for them to feed even themselves."

"What do they live on? And where do they find water?"

"I don't know. Perhaps she'll tell us in the morning."

"She'd better," said Ivo grimly. "We still have another day's journey ahead of us and less than a gourd of water to see us through."

"I'm sure she will," said Neva. "She was afraid of us to begin with, but she's not now."

The sun set, and wrapping themselves in their cloaks against the chill that came over the desert with the darkness, they stretched out on the sand at the foot of the rock. Ivo did not fall asleep at once but lay there for some time, looking up at the cold glitter of the stars and worrying about what was ahead of them. And when he did sleep it was lightly, uneasily.

Liall woke him, shaking him.

"What is it?" he asked, sitting up.

"The old woman's gone," said Liall.

It was some time before dawn, but there was enough light to see that this was true.

"That's not all," said Liall. "She stole my water gourd."

Neva was awake now, too.

"She couldn't have!" she said. "Are you sure?"

"Yes," said Liall. "It was tied to my belt, and it's gone."

"But how could she?" asked Neva. "We tried to help her, shared what we had with her."

Ivo shrugged. "You asked what kind of people drive their old away to die and Liall said the Hiltis. Well, she's a Hilti, and she probably cared no more about us than her people did about her. The question is, what we do now? Do you think we can follow and catch her?"

Liall shook his head. "There's no telling when she went or which way."

This was true, too. The wind that blew before dawn each day had covered her footprints.

"Then we'll have to go on without water," said

Ivo, "and hope we are out of the desert by nightfall."

"I can't think of anything else that we can do," said Liall.

Since none of them was hungry, they set off at once, going around the rocks and then westward. By the time the sun was completely up, they had left the rocks far behind them and were on a flat expanse of sand where they could travel at a good pace. On they went, talking little to save their strength. Ivo had been thirsty when he woke—his sleep had been full of dreams of clear running brooks that disappeared when he approached them—and as the sun climbed higher his mouth and throat became even more parched. He glanced at Neva. Her face was set and drawn, but her stride was as long as ever.

Several times during the morning they saw more *doranc*, but they saw nothing else.

When the sun was directly overhead, they paused.

"Shall we rest?" asked Neva.

"If you're not too tired, I think we should go on," said Ivo.

"I'm not tired," she said, and so they went on again. But now there was a faint shadow on her face and occasionally she licked her lips, which were almost as dry and cracked as the old woman's had been.

The sun beat down on them, and even with their hoods pulled well forward the glare reflected from the white sand hurt their eyes. The heat was so intense that every breath became painful, searing their lungs.

But they continued on, grimly, doggedly, as the sun moved on before them. Neva was not walking so steadily now. She stumbled once, and Ivo said, "Give me your basket."

She shook her head, but he took it from her and slung it next to his own. She smiled at him and then winced for even the slightest movement hurt her lips.

Looking up shortly after this, Ivo saw the vultures again. They were wheeling and circling almost directly overhead, and this time he knew who they were watching. He looked ahead, narrowing his eyes against the dazzle and hoping to see something besides the endless expanse of sand. But there was nothing except a line of reddish dunes with another clump of *doranc* near them.

And then Neva fell. Ivo and Liall both hurried to her and tried to pick her up, but she shook her head.

"No," she whispered. "I can't."

"Of course you can," said Ivo. He and Liall lifted her to her feet and they went on for a while with the two of them supporting her. Then she stumbled and fell again.

"I tell you I can't," she said. "Go on without me."

"Stop that, Neva!" said Ivo. "We're not going to leave you."

"If you don't, we'll all die. Couldn't you go on and see if you can get help or find some water?"

"No!" said Ivo. He was just lifting her to her feet again, intending to carry her, when Liall said, "Look!"

Another Hilti had appeared from behind the *doranc.* Though dressed like the old woman in a white robe, turban and veil, this was probably a man for he was taller than she had been and he carried a long spear. He seeemed to be stalking something, for he moved slowly and carefully, his spear poised. He threw it, then darted forward.

Putting Neva down, Ivo stumbled towards him. The spear had transfixed a large lizard, pinning it to the ground. Pulling the spear free, the Hilti turned to face Ivo.

"Help!" croaked Ivo. "You must help us."

"Help?" He looked at Ivo blankly.

"Yes. My sister is dying."

The Hilti glanced at Neva, who was lying where Ivo had left her on the hot sand. Only his eyes were visible above the white veil, but their expression changed as if he were smiling.

"Good," he said. "It is almost a moon since I have seen anyone die."

Chapter 7

Ivo stared at him.

"What did you say?"

"I said it is almost a moon since I have seen anyone die."

Throwing back his head he gave a long, wailing call, then picked up the lizard and walked to where Neva was lying. Dazed and certain that he had not understood him, Ivo stumbled after him. Liall, kneeling beside Neva, looked up at the Hilti.

"How long since she ate?" asked the Hilti.

"Last night," said Liall.

"Oh," said the Hilti, disappointed. "Then it will take a long time—at least another few days."

"What will take a long time?" asked Liall.

"Until she dies," said the Hilti. "Unless you would like me to kill her for you. Would you?"

Liall stared at him as incredulously as Ivo had.

"Are you mad?" he asked.

The Hilti blinked. "Of course not," he said. "It is wrong to kill one of your own. But she is nothing to me, and I will be glad to do it for you."

Liall looked at him, then at Ivo.

"He *is* mad," he said.

"No," said Ivo. "He said something almost as unbelievable as that to me."

"But we don't want her to die!" said Liall. "We want to save her!"

Now it was the Hilti who looked astonished.

"Why?" he asked.

"Because she's Ivo's sister and my good friend! And even if she wasn't . . . Will you help us or not?"

"It is you who are mad," said the Hilti. "Why should I help you? Whenever someone dies there is that much more food for everyone else."

Again Liall looked at Ivo.

"It's no use," said Ivo.

"I can see that," said Liall. "What shall we do?"

"Carry her," said Ivo. "I'll take her."

"No," said Liall. "Let me."

Struggling to his feet, he lifted Neva to his shoulder, then paused. Probably in answer to the Hilti's call, three more of the veiled and white robed nomads had appeared, one of them coming from behind the *doranc*, the other two from the far side of the dune. Like the man who had killed the lizard, they all carried spears.

"What is it, Harnac?" asked one of them.

"Strangers from outside," said the first Hilti. "They say the woman is dying."

"Then why are they carrying her?"

"Because, in spite of all of you, we're going to save her!" said Ivo.

Liall, with Neva over his shoulder, was starting to trudge off.

"Come on, Ivo," he said.

"Yes," said Ivo. The Hilti they had called Harnac was standing in front of him. "Get out of my way!"

Harnac did not move.

"Why are you being so foolish?" he said. "If you put her down, we can all watch her die together. If you don't . . ."

Sick with rage and despair, Ivo pushed him aside; pushed him so hard that he staggered and almost fell.

The other three Hiltis sighed softly.

"Who called?" said a voice behind Ivo. "Was it you, Harnac?"

"Yes," he said. "Strangers. One of them is dying. Now this one will die too."

Turning, Ivo saw that several more Hiltis had appeared. They were standing in a half-circle behind him.

"He attacked Harnac," said one of the original

three. "Pushed him. Do not kill him too quickly, Harnac."

"It may be that that is what he wants," said Harnac. "Is it?" he asked. "Or do you want to fight?"

Ivo looked at him without answering.

"I don't think he understands," said one of the Hiltis behind Ivo.

"He understands," said Harnac. "He talked to me."

Raising his spear he prodded Ivo gently in the chest, the sharp flint point just touching the skin.

"Which will it be, fight or die?"

"Fight," said Ivo.

Unslinging his basket and Neva's, he dropped them. Liall, with Neva over his shoulder, had paused about a dozen yards away.

"Go on, Liall."

"No," said Liall.

"You must!"

"No," said Liall again. "We can't trust them. I'll guard your back." And lowering Neva to the sand, he drew his sword and came back towards Ivo, taking his stand behind him.

"Why is he guarding him?" asked one of the Hiltis near him. "This is between the light-haired one and Harnac."

"Yes," said Harnac. Then to Ivo, "Well?"

Ivo drew his sword also. His throat was so dry that he could not swallow, but he no longer felt weak: he was too angry. He knew, however, that he must control that anger and that he must end the fight quickly for he had no reserves for a long engagement.

He poised himself, sword ready, watching Harnac. Was he going to throw his spear? If he did, Ivo had little chance for he had no buckler. If he didn't . . .

He didn't. Circling him, Harnac's spear darted out, and Ivo parried his thrust, deliberately holding back and making the parry seem a little clumsy. Harnac's dark eyes narrowed slightly, and Ivo knew that again he was smiling under the white veil. He feinted, then like a striking snake drove the spear at Ivo's chest. Again Ivo warded it off, then struck—not at Harnac but at the spear—shearing through the shaft so that the flint head dropped to the sand, then bringing his blade around and up and driving the spear high in the air. Arms raised, Harnac staggered back, tripped and fell. Almost before his shoulders touched the sand, Ivo was standing over him, the point of his sword at his throat.

Again the watching Hiltis sighed.

"Do you yield?" asked Ivo.

"Yield?"

"Yes. Have you had enough?"

"You mean you're not going to kill me?"

"I'm not a Hilti!"

"He *can* talk," said the man who stood just behind Ivo. "But what he says makes no more sense than what he does."

"No," said another. "Well, at least I shall eat."

And he picked up Harnac's lizard.

"Why should you have it?"

"Because I was the first one here."

"I will take this," said another, picking up the flint head of Harnac's spear. "It is a better one than mine. We will be watching the vultures," he said to Harnac. "We will see you again when they begin gathering." Then he and the others moved off, each going his separate way.

Slowly Harnac got to his feet.

"I don't understand," he said. "Why didn't you kill me?"

"I told you why," said Ivo. "We're not Hiltis, and we don't believe in killing." He sheathed his sword. "You take the baskets," he said to Liall. "I'll take Neva."

"You're going?" said Harnac.

"Yes."

"But if you want to save the girl, why don't you let her drink first?"

"How can we? We have no water."

"Why do you need water? There is a *doranc*."

"What?"

"You don't know how to get drink from a *doranc*? Carry her over there."

Puzzled, Ivo picked Neva up. Her eyes opened.

"Ivo, you mustn't . . ." she whispered hoarsely.

"Ssh," he said and carried her to where Harnac was waiting next to the tall, thorny plant.

"Golka took my spear point," said Harnac. "Give me your weapon."

Ivo hesitated.

"Here, take mine," said Liall, who had followed them. He drew his sword and gave it to him. Harnac thrust it into the thickest part of the *doranc*, then took a short length of hollow reed from inside his robe and pushed it into the hole.

"Drink," he said.

Neva had been watching, and when Ivo set her down she put her mouth to the end of the reed and sucked, tentatively at first and then eagerly.

"Then there is water here?" said Liall.

"The *doranc* only grows where there is water," said Harnac. "It is deep under the sand, too deep to dig, but the roots find it."

Finally, with a sigh, Neva took her mouth from the reed.

"Is there more there?" asked Ivo.

She nodded.

"Go ahead, Liall."

He watched as Liall drank, then bent over the reed himself and drew on it. The water the plant had stored was warm and rather sweet, but it tasted as delicious to him as the clearest spring water. When he had had enough, he straightened up.

"Thank you, Harnac," he said.

"What does that mean?"

"It means we're grateful to you," said Neva.

"I don't know what that means either," said Harnac. "What will you do now?"

"Go on to the west," said Ivo. "And you?"

"I will wait here to die."

"Why must you die?" asked Liall.

"I have no spear. How will I get food or protect myself?"

"Can't you make another spear?" asked Ivo.

"The stones for the points come from the hills to the west. And since I have no food I would die before I could get there and back again."

"How far is it to the hills?"

"A day's journey. But I have not eaten for several days now."

Ivo exchanged glances with Neva and Liall.

"We are going to the hills," he said. "Why don't you come with us? We have food, and we will protect you."

"You will give me food? Why?"

"I told you why twice," said Ivo. "We do not believe in killing, and we do believe in helping others when we can."

"Even though I tried to kill you?"

"In the end, you helped us," said Liall. "You showed us how to get water from the *doranc*. Will you come?"

"I have never heard of people like you," said Harnac. "It has always been said that those who live to the north and south of Morven hate everyone, one another even more than us. But if you mean it, I will come."

"Good," said Ivo. He looked west to where the sun was about to set and then at Neva. "How are you feeling now?"

"Much better," she said. "If I can rest for a while, I'll be ready to go on."

"Then I think we should eat now and then go."

"At night?"

"If you do not need to hunt for food, that is the best time to travel," said Harnac. "It is not so hot and the others will not see us."

"You think they will attack us?" asked Liall.

"Not if we are all together and they know that you have weapons."

"We not only have them but if we need to use them, we will," said Ivo.

They ate there by the *doranc*, sharing their faring-bread with Harnac. Though he praised it, saying it was as good food as he had ever eaten and though he was clearly very hungry, he ate very little of it. Then they all drank from the *doranc* again and, as it became dark, they set off.

Harnac led the way, guiding himself by the stars. He set a fast pace—Ivo was afraid it was too fast for Neva—but she insisted that it was not and so they pressed on over the sand that gleamed white in the faint light of the stars.

They rested once at about midnight, then went on

again. And when the sun rose, they saw the Wendery Hills ahead of them.

The hills were still some distance off, dark against the sky. Though they were all tired, now that the end of their journey was in sight, they decided to press on. And by midmorning they had left the sandy waste behind them and were on the rocky but green slopes that led up to the hills.

Chapter 8

The sound of running water led them up the rocky slope to the banks of a rushing stream. They were no longer desperately thirsty, but the memory of what they had been through was still so vivid that Neva, Ivo and Liall knelt beside it and drank. The water, coming from somewhere high in the hills, was clear and very cold.

"Is that water?" asked Harnac.

"Yes, of course," said Ivo. "Why?"

"I have never seen so much of it. Where does it come from, and where does it go?"

"It comes from up there," said Liall. "And since it goes north from here it probably ends up in the sea."

Harnac knelt and drank also, somewhat cautiously at first.

"It's good," he said. "Better than the water in the *doranc*."

"You've never been here before?" asked Neva.

"No."

"Then where did you get the flint for your spear?"

"From my father, who got it from his father," said Harnac. "My drinking reed I got myself where we all get them: from a foul-smelling green place over there." And he nodded towards the south.

"There is a marsh there near the edge of the desert," said Liall. "Where will you get your flint?"

"I don't know."

"Let's try up there," said Ivo.

They went farther up the slope and found a ledge that had many flints in it, some still embedded in the softer rock, some lying loose on the ground. While Harnac searched for one of suitable size and shape, Ivo went to a small copse of ash and cut down a stout, straight sapling, trimming it and notching the end with his sword.

"Here," he said, giving it to Harnac.

Harnac glanced at him, then took it and fitted a sharp, flat flint into the notch, tying it in place with strips of dried lizard skin.

"It is a good spear," he said, trying its balance. "Better than my old one."

"You are going now?" asked Neva.

"Yes," he said. "I know how to live in the desert,

where to find food and water. I would not know how to live here."

He looked at them each in turn, his eyes speculative and a little puzzled. Then, shrugging, he turned and went back down the slope towards the desert.

"A strange man," said Liall.

"A strange people," said Neva. "At one time I would have said evil. But now, considering where and how they live and who lives on either side of them, I don't know."

"We in Andor are not evil," said Liall.

"You hate no one?" asked Neva.

"I can't say I like those in Brunn."

"And the others in your country hate them," said Neva. "And those in Brunn hate you enough to kill you on sight. Surrounded by this and living as they do, is it any wonder that the Hiltis are what they are?"

"Perhaps not," said Liall thoughtfully. Then to Ivo who was hunting among the flints that were lying near the ledge, "What are you looking for?"

"A striking stone. When we get up into the hills, we'll need a fire."

He found one he liked, put it in the pouch on his belt, and then they went on up the slope towards the hills, following the stream.

They climbed steadily all day, over scree slopes and through narrow valleys, towards Tarec, the tallest of the peaks that towered above them to the west. By dusk they were in a rocky pass high in the hills. The stream was only a rill now and finding a shallow cave that would give them some protection from the wind, they decided to spend the night there. As Ivo had expected, it was much colder in the hills than on the desert, and while Neva and Liall gathered wood, he used the flint he had picked up and the blade of his sword to strike sparks into a handful of dry moss. He fed the flames with small twigs, and when Neva and Liall returned with wood, he added that carefully until they had a roaring fire.

"This bread is good," said Liall as they took some of the flat cakes from their baskets. "But I wish we had something hot to go with it."

"It may be that we have," said Neva.

Digging down to the bottom of her basket, she took out a packet of dried herbs and an earthenware pot, which she filled with water from the rill and set on the fire. When the water boiled, she sprinkled some of the herbs into it. An aromatic smell filled the cave, and when they drank the infusion, they found that it not only warmed and cheered them but lessened their fatigue.

Partially covering the fire with earth so that it would burn all night, they wrapped themselves in their cloaks and slept. They had reason to be glad that they had found the cave to sleep in, for shortly before dawn a violent storm broke. It began with wind that whistled through the pass, making the fire leap and flicker. Then lightning flashed and thunder roared

Chadron State College Library
Chadron, Nebraska

and the rain came down in sheets, turning the rill into a raging torrent. They had brought wood into the cave with them, and they built up the fire and brewed more of the herb tea to have with the faring-bread when they broke their fast. Though it was violent, the storm did not last long, and when it was over they slung their baskets and started on again.

The pass took them to the foot of Tarec but at this point there was no way up it for it rose sheer in a rock wall. They went south along the base of the cliff, looking for a place where they could climb it. As they picked their way over the rough ground and between the large rocks that lay at the foot of the cliff, they heard a strange sound that was half screech and half squawk. Something moved near the cliff face and when they approached it they saw that it was an eaglet, too young to fly. It glared at them, flapping its dark wings, as they drew near it, but otherwise it did not move.

"It must have fallen from its nest or been blown from it in the storm," said Ivo.

"Yes," said Liall. "There it is." And he pointed to a ledge about a hundred feet up the cliff where they could see a tangle of sticks.

"What are we going to do about it?" asked Neva.

"Why must we do anything?" asked Ivo.

"We can't leave it here. It will die or be killed. Couldn't you put it back into its nest?"

"I don't know," said Ivo, looking at the sheer face

of the cliff. "I can climb a tree, but I don't see how anyone can climb that."

"There's a chimney," said Liall, nodding to a crack that ran up the face of the cliff, passing close to the ledge. "I think I might be able to get up that."

"Will you try?" asked Neva.

"If it would please you, yes," he said smiling.

Taking off her cloak, Neva talked softly and soothingly to the bird, then threw the cloak over it. She picked it up, wrapping it carefully in the cloak, and held it while Liall took off his cloak also. He put the bird inside his tunic, then edged sideways into the crack and began working his way up, pressing his feet against one side of the cleft and his back against the other. When he was some sixty or seventy feet up, the crack narrowed and he turned to face the cliff and continued on, finding foot- and handholds on the inside surfaces of the crack.

He paused when he was slightly above the ledge, leaning out to see how he could get on to it from the crack. As he did, a shadow fell on him, and looking up Neva and Ivo saw a dark shape diving down on him from high above. It was the male eagle, enraged at what he took to be an assault on the nest. Down he came, the wind whistling through his plumage, talons extended.

Then, as he was about to strike, Neva screamed. It was not an expression of fear, but the kind of scream the eagle might have uttered himself in calling to his mate. The huge bird, wings spread wide, veered away from Liall and began circling overhead. Neva looked up at him and though she did not make another sound, Ivo sensed that she was speaking to him. He made another circle, then landed on the ledge and waited there, his fierce, curved beak slightly open.

"It's all right, Liall," called Neva. "I told him what you were doing. He won't hurt you."

Liall, who had flattened himself against the cliff, looked down at her and then at the eagle.

"Are you sure?"

"Yes," she said. She looked up at the eagle, and he moved off slightly to the far side of the nest.

Tentatively, eyes on the bird, Liall stepped on to the ledge. Reaching into the breast of his tunic, he took out the cloak, unfolded it and put the eaglet into the nest. The young bird flapped its wings and screeched again, and the large male bent down as if to quiet it and also make sure that it was unhurt.

Tucking Neva's cloak into his tunic, Liall stepped back into the crack and began to make his way back down again.

"How did you do that?" asked Ivo.

"I don't know."

"You don't?"

"No. I just knew I could talk to him, and I did."

"And you don't know where or how you learned to do it?"

"No."

"I wonder if I can do it, too."

"Somehow I don't think so."

By this time Liall had reached the base of the cliff.

"Thank you," he said, giving Neva back her cloak.

"I'm sorry you had a bad moment there," she said.

"Not one. Several." He waited, watching Neva as she stood there looking up at the eagle. "What is he saying now?"

"He told me his name. It's Akala. And he thanks us."

"Ask him how we can get to the top of Tarec," said Ivo.

"I did. And he said the best way is just ahead of us, a little farther to the south. But he doesn't think we should go up there."

"Why not?"

"Because there's something dangerous there."

"Did he say what?"

"No. He just said it's large and fierce."

"Then the tales that are told about Tarec are true," said Liall.

"What tales?" asked Neva.

"That it is not only a sacred mountain, forbidden, but that there is a watcher there, guarding the summit."

"But we've got to go up," said Ivo.

"I told him that," said Neva. "And he said he'd go with us and if he can help us he will."

"Interesting," said Liall, picking up his basket.

"He's a bird, not a man, but he knows the meaning of the words thanks and help when Harnac didn't."

They set off again along the base of the cliff, and as they moved, Akala flapped his wings and began circling again, flying higher and higher until he was just a dark dot in the clear blue sky. They soon came to the place he meant: a fault or break in the cliff. They went into it and found that though the rock here was steep and covered with fragments, they could make their way up it. The climbing was difficult and slow, for the scree slid under their feet, but they struggled on and when they finally came out of the fault they were above the cliff and could see the top of Tarec ahead of them.

They stood there for a moment, looking up, and Liall shivered.

"Can you feel it?" he asked.

"I can feel the wind," said Ivo. "A cold, biting wind."

"It's not just the wind," said Neva. "There's something else here—something that does not want us to go any farther."

"But we must," said Ivo. "If Liall is right and we do not, we will not only be abandoning our quest but losing a chance to lift the spell that was put on us."

"I did not say we should not go on," said Liall. "I just think, though the way is clear, that it will not be easy."

"Has any part of it been easy so far?" asked Ivo.

"No," said Liall. "Forward then." And pulling their cloaks more closely about them, they started up the slope. The wind tore at them, holding them back, and now Ivo began to feel what Neva and Liall had sensed: some inimical force that bore down on them, making every plodding step an effort; something chill and inhuman that worked not only on their bodies but on their spirits, saying, "Who are you to dare this climb? Think you that your quest—any of your aspirations—has any real meaning? There is nothing here—nothing anywhere. There is no future as there is no past. Life is as unsubstantial as the morning mist and nothing endures."

Several times Ivo was on the point of giving up. Why should they struggle this way? Even if their quest was successful, would it have any significance in the great scale of things? And if they were nothing, then why should it matter that they did not know who they were?

Looking at Neva and Liall, he knew that they felt as he did but still they went on, teeth clenched, something inside them burning like a carefully shielded candle flame, making them fight their way up the barren slope.

It took them most of the morning to reach a rock wall that rose almost vertically to Tarec's peak. Then the wind died. They were no longer oppressed by the force that had been holding them back. There was silence except for their labored breathing.

This last pitch was so steep that they had to help one another up it. When they were just below the top, Ivo said, "Wait here."

"Why?" asked Liall.

"You said yourself that there was something there—something dangerous—and so did Akala."

"All the more reason why I should come, too."

"Very well. But not you, Neva. Wait until we call you."

She hesitated, then nodded. Drawing their swords, Ivo and Liall climbed the last few feet and found themselves on a plateau that was several hundred yards across. It was dotted with large, weathered rocks as the slopes below had been, but in the center was one that looked as if it had been worked by man; a smooth black stone that was lying on the ground.

Swords in hands, Ivo and Liall looked around. There was nothing else, nothing that moved.

"Well?" said Neva.

"There doesn't seem to be anything here," said Ivo.

"Then I'm coming up, too."

Again Ivo looked around, then sheathing his sword, he held out his hand to her. As he drew her up beside him, he heard Liall gasp and, turning, felt his heart leap, then clench with fear. A monster had appeared from behind one of the large rocks on the far side of the plateau and was glaring at them.

It was a creature out of a nightmare: many times the size of a horse with three heads and a greenish body covered with scales. It had batlike wings and its talons were sharp and hooked; they scraped on the rock as it launched itself at them, jaws agape.

Without thinking and without knowing why he did it, Ivo turned sideways, raising his left fist threateningly and swinging his right hand back with the forefinger pointing down. The monster had begun a rumbling roar as it came towards them, but now that changed to a hoarse scream. Extending its wings, it rose into the air, passing just over their heads, then wheeled and flew off towards the south.

Ivo remained rigid, aware that Neva had taken the same stance he had, until the monster disappeared in the distance.

Liall, standing between them, was the first to move or make a sound. He let out his breath in a long sigh.

"It seems to be gone," he said. "Will it come back?"

"No," said Neva.

Liall looked at her and then at Ivo, and it was clear that he wanted to ask her how she knew and how both of them had known what to do. But he didn't. And it was just as well, because Ivo would not have been able to answer and he didn't think Neva could either.

Chapter 9

"Where is the stone?" asked Neva.

"I think over there," said Ivo.

For a moment none of them moved, held back—not by fear—but by a feeling of awe. For this was something out of time—set there they did not know when or by whom—that they hoped would speak to them from the distant past. More than that, if it had a message for them then this quest of theirs must have been forseen, and they suddenly had a sense that everything they had done and hoped to do was part of a larger pattern that they could not as yet begin to understand.

Slowly, aware of what was at stake, they picked their way between the rocks that lay about the plateau and looked down at the stone. As Ivo had thought when he had first caught a glimpse of it, the rock had clearly been shaped by human hands. It was a stele or tablet about four feet long and two feet wide and about four inches thick with a rounded top. The base on which it had stood was of the same black stone. And though both were time-worn and weathered, it seemed probable that the whole had not fallen but had been struck down, for it was split vertically, there was a piece missing from the top and the bottom was completely shattered. What was dismaying about it, however, was that the stone was smooth and blank.

"Perhaps this is the back," said Liall. "Let's turn it over."

Lifting each half separately and carefully, they turned them over and fitted them together again. And there was something on the other side; a bas-relief at the top and what seemed to be an inscription below it.

There were three figures in the bas-relief. Though worn by the scouring wind, two of them seemed to be a man and a woman, both naked, holding hands. Behind and above them stood a third robed figure with hands extended over their heads as if in blessing. It was hard to tell if this was a man or a woman, for this part of the stone was broken, but Ivo had a feeling that it was a woman.

"Do you know who they are, Liall?" asked Neva.

"No. I had never heard of the stone before this

quest was given to us. And all I know about Tarec is that none are supposed to come here, for it was from here that Kennar, who founded Andor, had his first sight of the land."

"Perhaps this is Kennar," said Ivo, pointing to the naked man.

"Perhaps," said Liall.

They now looked at the inscription that was sharper and clearer than the three figures, but even more puzzling. For the characters were not those used in the Common speech but they did not seem to be those of the Tree alphabet either.

"Can you make it out, Neva?" asked Ivo.

"No."

"They seem to be runes," said Liall. "If they are and we cannot read them, then we have made this journey for nothing."

There was a sudden flapping behind them and they turned, thinking it was Akala. But it was not. It was a gore-crow, larger than any they had seen on the dead horses in the Burnt Place. It had settled on one of the large rocks and was watching them with sharp, beady eyes.

"What is it doing here?" asked Liall.

"Perhaps it lives here," said Ivo.

"Crows do not nest this high nor in rocky places like this," said Liall. He studied it uneasily. "Can you talk to it, Neva?"

She looked fixedly at the crow as she had at Akala,

and it stared back at her. Finally she shook her head.

"I think it understood me, but it would not answer."

"Well, it cannot harm us," said Ivo. "But what shall we do about the inscription?"

"If we copied it we might find someone who could read it," said Liall.

"Who?" asked Ivo.

"Zothar, High Steward of Andor, is very wise and learned in ancient lore. If anyone can read it, he can."

"Wait," said Neva who had been frowning at the inscription. "Ivo, give me your sword."

He glanced at her, puzzled, then drew it and gave it to her. She held it out over the stone, looking—not at the stone itself—but at its reflection in the bright blade. Ivo leaned forward, looking at it too, then said, "It *is* in the Tree alphabet!"

"Yes," said Neva. "I thought that it looked familiar except that the characters slanted the wrong way. It's reversed, as if written in a mirror."

"Then you can read it?" said Liall.

"I think so." She adjusted the angle, looking at the reflection of the characters in the steel. " 'Andor and Brunn,' " she said slowly, " 'shall again be one when Ima . . .' " and she paused.

"Ima what?" asked Liall.

"There's a gap there," said Neva. "Something's missing. The next word is 'marries.' Then the rest is missing, too."

" 'Andor and Brunn shall again be one,' " said Liall,

" 'when Ima something marries something.' "

"That's right," said Ivo. "Does that mean anything to you?"

"No," said Liall. "It is said that once, many centuries ago, Andor and Brunn were one land under one king. But beyond that I know nothing."

"Not even who Ima is?" asked Neva.

"No."

"The missing pieces of the stone must still be here," said Ivo. "If we can find them and fit them in that might help us to understand what it means."

"It might," said Liall.

Neva gave Ivo back his sword and all three of them began hunting through the fragments of rock that lay about the shattered stone. They found several shards that had been broken from it, but they were all part of the back or sides and had no characters on them.

"Could they be underneath the stone?" asked Neva. "After all, we moved it."

"That's true," said Liall.

Together they slid the broken pieces of the stone aside and went on looking.

"Wait," said Ivo, spying a flat, black flake, a little smaller than his hand, that was lying in a crack. "I think . . ."

He reached for it. And as he did the gore-crow dropped from the rock on which it had been sitting, seized the fragment in its beak and flapped off with it.

"Hoy!" shouted Ivo angrily. "Come back here!" And picking up a stone he threw it at the bird. But the crow dodged and continued, flying southeast.

"I knew I did not like it," said Liall. "What do we do now?"

"I don't know," said Ivo, staring after the bird. "I'm sure it was one of the pieces we wanted. There were characters on it and . . ."

He broke off as Neva, looking up, screamed shrilly as she had before. In a few moments Akala, who had been flying so high above them that he was invisible, came diving down. When he was a score of yards over their heads, he began circling while Neva again spoke soundlessly to him, then he flew off towards the southeast also.

"What did you say to him?" asked Liall.

"I asked him to follow the crow and, if he could, take the stone from him. If not, to tell us where he went and what he did with it."

"I can't say I liked climbing to his nest before," said Liall, "but from now on I shall never question any request you may make. Is there anything we can do while we wait?"

"There were two fragments of the stone missing," said Ivo. "We should make sure we haven't overlooked the other one."

And so they searched again, combing the rocky surface of the plateau, not only around the broken stone and its base, but over a wider area. But they found nothing.

Then Akala returned, slanting down from on high and settling with outstretched wings on the same rock on which the gore-crow had sat when he was watching them.

He fixed his fierce eye on Neva, and she returned his gaze.

"What does he say?" asked Ivo.

"He could not catch the crow and take the stone from him, but he saw where he went."

"Where?"

"To a walled city with many towers near a wide river."

"That would be Lantar," said Liall with some excitement. "Where in the city did he go?"

"He does not know. But he was almost on him when they reached the city and the crow, trying to avoid him, flew low over a courtyard with a fountain and dropped the stone. And a man picked it up; a tall man in a dark robe."

"Did he have a beard?"

"Yes. A short grey beard."

"Zothar!" said Liall. "If it was he, then all is well. For he will give it to us if we ask him for it."

"Then you think we should go to this Lantar of yours?"

"If we want to find out what the missing words in the inscription are, yes."

"I do not know how that will help us," said Neva. "Even if he gets that piece there is still another one missing."

Though she spoke quietly, there was a note of despair in her voice that made Liall look at her sharply.

"But it will tell us something," he said. "Are you thinking of the journey back across Morven?"

She shook her head.

"Then what is it?"

She shrugged and Ivo said, "You suggested—and we both hoped—that if we found the stone the spell might be lifted. But it has not been."

"You still remember nothing?"

"No more than I did on the heath. Do you, Neva?"

"No."

"I'm sorry," said Liall. "To me, of course, you are what you have always been."

"And what is that?" she asked in the same flat, hopeless voice. "How can I be anything when I don't know who or what I was? I feel I am nothing, no one."

"Neva," said Ivo. He put an arm around her, and this time she did not pull away from him but leaned against him.

"I still think that the spell has some connection with our quest," said Liall. "And if that is so, then could it not be that it will not be lifted until we have read and understood what was written on the stone?"

"That might well be," said Ivo.

"I suppose it might," said Neva with an effort. "In any case, if we have nothing else, we have the task that was given us. So we will go to Lantar with you."

"Good," said Liall. "As for Morven, I have a thought. There are marshes south of the hills, the ones Harnac spoke of. If Akala can guide us across them, we will not have to go back the way we came."

"I'll ask him," said Neva. She turned to the eagle once more. "He says he will. He'll be watching, and he'll meet us when we're at the marshes."

Akala spread his wings and flew off. They went to the edge of the plateau and stood there for a few moments looking about them. East, beyond the lower peaks of the hills, was Morven, its sand gleaming white in the noonday sun. North were the plains of Brunn, stretching league after league till they met the faint, shimmering blue that was the sea. South was Andor, its plains more rolling than those of Brunn with a range of snow capped mountains behind them. It was there, Liall told them, that the River Mendir rose, winding across the plain until it reached the hills and was lost in the marshes just below them.

"How far is it to Lantar?" asked Ivo.

"About three days by foot," said Liall. "Too far to see from here. It lies there where the Mendir curves due south."

They looked where he was pointing, and it was true. They could see nothing but the green plains that blended with the sky in the distance. Then they started their descent. The force that had made every step of their climb up Tarec so difficult did not seem to affect them now, and they worked their way slowly and carefully down the steep upper slopes, going back through the fault in the cliff and then turning south. The hills were not quite as rocky here as they were to the east, and by dusk they had reached the foot of the hills, and the Mendir Marshes were ahead of them.

They camped that night near a stream that came down from the hills and emptied into the marshes. In the morning they looked out over the green expanse that was dotted with reed-fringed pools.

"You think we can cross that?" asked Ivo dubiously.

"Akala seemed to think we could," said Neva. "In any case, I would rather try it than go into the desert again."

"Very well," said Ivo, remembering what had happened there. "Where is Akala?"

"He's coming," said Neva. "There." And she nodded to where the great bird was descending in wide circles. He soared overhead for a moment, then flew off to the right.

"This way," said Neva, and they set off along the edge of the marshes. About a quarter of a mile farther on, they came to a point that ran out towards the center of the marshes. The ground was firm here, though there were rushes on both sides of it and large areas of evil-smelling mud. There was open water at the end of the point but beyond that there was even higher ground; an island on which swamp oak and alder grew. It was perhaps fifty yards away but what could be seen of the bottom was sandy rather than muddy and appeared to be safe enough. Ivo insisted on going first and found that he could wade across easily enough though in one place the water came up to his waist.

Neva and Liall joined him and when they had forced their way through the trees and brush of the island to the far side, they found Akala waiting for them, hovering overhead on outstretched wings. Again he pointed out the best routes to them, and so, wading from island to island and in only one place finding it necessary to swim, they made their way across the marshes, reaching the other side shortly after noon.

Akala circled above them once more. They waved their thanks and farewell to him, and then he flew off over the marsh and back towards his eyrie on the cliff below Tarec.

They sat for a while on the bank at the edge of the marshes, eating the last of the dried fruit that they had in their baskets and letting their clothes dry in the warm sun. Then they began their march eastward over the rolling plain.

"You say that it will take us three days to get to Lantar?" said Ivo.

"A bit less than that from here," said Liall. "Why?"

"I'm not sure we have enough of the faring-bread to last us until then."

"We're not in Morven now," said Liall. "We're in Andor. We're sure to come on a farm or cattle-herder's stead, if not by nightfall, then sometime tomorrow."

"We may not have to wait until then to meet someone," said Neva. "Aren't those horses?"

Ivo and Liall shaded their eyes, looking in the direction she was pointing; a little south of west.

"Yes!" said Liall. Taking his cloak from his basket, he flourished it, swinging it high in the air, and at once the horsemen in the distance changed their direction and came galloping towards them.

There were half a dozen of them, all warriors, for even at a distance Ivo could see the gleam of their helmets, byrnies and bucklers. When they were close enough, he saw that their leader was only a little older than Liall; a broad-shouldered, brown-haired young man.

"Gildar!" called Liall as the horsemen drew up before them.

The young warrior stared at him. Then, with a shout, he leaped from his saddle.

"Prince!" he said, sinking to one knee. "This is as joyous and unexpected a sight as any I ever did see! You are alive then?"

"Not only alive, but well. Nay, kneel not to me." And he lifted him to his feet and embraced him.

"But how is that possible?" asked Gildar. "One of

Rendel's men brought word that you had been struck down, and it was thought, if you were not slain, that you were a captive in Brunn."

"It is possible because my two friends here saved me," said Liall. "But what do you in these parts, so far from Lantar?"

"I rode here to raise a levy among the horsemen of Westfell."

"A levy? For a war gathering?"

"What else after what happened—or what the king thought had happened—at the border?"

"So," said Liall turning a troubled face to Neva and Ivo, "while we were searching for a way to bring peace to Andor and Brunn, swords were being sharpened." He turned back to Gildar. "We must get to Lantar as soon as possible. Do you have three horses that can carry double?"

"All of them can," said Gildar. "But they will not have to do so for long. There is a farm less than a league from here. We can get horses for you there."

"Then let us ride," said Liall. Gildar held the stirrup while Liall mounted, then swung up behind him. Two of the other horsemen took up Neva and Ivo and they went galloping off eastward.

Chapter 10

"Yes," said Liall, pulling up his horse. "That is Lantar."

It was the afternoon of the next day. As Gildar had said, they had been able to get horses at a farm a few miles from the place where they had met him and had spent the night at a second, larger farm. They had made an early start, ridden hard all day and were now only a few miles from the walled town.

"I think, Prince, that the king should be told that you are coming," said Gildar.

"Perhaps," said Liall. "Who will you send?"

Gildar looked over his company, picked the man-at-arms whose horse seemed the least tired and sent him on ahead while the rest of them followed more slowly.

They were on a tree-lined road that wound through fields of ripening grain. There were stone farm houses with thatched roofs near the road, comfortable and pleasant to look at, but Neva and Ivo were more interested in many-towered Lantar that lay ahead of them on the far side of the river. They agreed that it was strange to look at it and not know if they had ever been there before. Liall said he was sure that they had not; that if they had he would have known it; but they did not see how he could be certain. On the other hand, if he was right, Ivo said, it might well be the first time they had ever set eyes on anything larger than a village.

As they went on, the fields gave way to meadows where cattle and horses grazed. They rode over a bridge, through the open gates of the town where they were saluted by men-at-arms, then along a narrow street into a square. There were houses and shops on three sides of it and the townspeople and merchants who had gathered there cheered when they appeared, and Liall smiled and waved in answer.

On the far side of the square was the palace. There were low steps in front of it, and on the steps, flanked by armed guards, were two men. One of them, tall, imposing, no longer young but still vigorous, wore a purple tunic and was clearly the king, Liall's uncle. The other was tall also, but somewhat stooped. He wore a dark robe with a gold chain around his neck and had a short grey beard. From what both Akala and

Liall had said, Ivo took him to be Zothar, High Steward of Andor.

Dismounting, Liall ran up the steps.

"Greetings, uncle," he said.

"Then it is true," said the king. "You are not only alive but unhurt?"

"Yes, uncle. Thanks to my two friends here."

"When Gildar's messenger brought me the news, I could not believe it." Then his stern, lined face relaxed, and he embraced Liall. "Welcome home, Liall."

"Thank you, uncle."

"May I welcome you too, Prince?" said Zothar. "I told his majesty that he should not give up hope for you, but he would not believe me either."

"Is that strange in the light of all that has happened?" asked the king.

"Perhaps not. But now that he is here, safe and well . . ."

"Nothing is changed!" said the king. Then he looked at Neva and Ivo who had dismounted also and were standing at the foot of the steps. "These are the two who saved you?"

"Yes, uncle," said Liall and bringing them to the king, he made them known to him.

"I will say nothing but thanks now," said the king. "Later, when I have heard the full tale, I will say and do much more. Rooms have been made ready for them, Liall, close to yours. Take them there, and we shall meet again when we dine in the great hall."

Ivo bowed to the king, and he and Neva followed Liall into the palace and up the broad stone steps to the sleeping chambers. Liall showed Neva into one of them and took Ivo to the one next to it. It was a large room, richly furnished and with tapestries on the walls. A shirt of white linen and a blue tunic and hose —Liall's by the look of them—lay on the bed, and there was a pair of low boots on the floor near them. Stripping off his clothes, Ivo washed at the large basin in the corner and dressed himself in the garments that had been put there for him. Then, going out into the corridor, he knocked on the door of Neva's room.

"Come in," she said.

He opened the door, then paused, staring. Neva had changed her clothes also. Instead of the grey, travel-stained tunic she had been wearing, she now had on a long crimson gown embroidered in gold. And instead of letting her tawny hair hang loose she had braided it and twisted the plaits around her head like a coronet.

"What are you staring at?" she asked.

"You."

"Why?"

"Because you look . . ." He hesitated.

"Yes?"

"Different." He had wanted to say beautiful but somehow he couldn't.

"Why shouldn't I when I'm wearing something

I've never worn before?"

"Because it's not just the dress."

"Don't you like it?"

"Of course I do. It's a beautiful dress."

"It's not the dress that's beautiful," said Liall from the doorway behind Ivo.

"Thank you, Liall," said Neva. "Did you choose it?"

"No. One of my mother's tiring women must have. And she must have had second sight. For the crimson makes your eyes look like sea emeralds and your hair like a king's treasure."

"It must indeed be a magical gown then," said Neva dryly. "Though its magic does not seem to work on everyone. Have you come to take us downstairs?"

"If you're ready."

"We are. At least, I am," said Neva and she took his arm and they went out and down the stairs with Ivo, feeling awkward and annoyed at his awkwardness, following them.

It was now dusk, but the great hall was bright with torches and tapers. The king was already sitting at the high table and he made much of Neva and Ivo when Liall brought them in and sat Neva on his right and Ivo on his left with Liall and Zothar on either side of them. Gildar was at the high table too, for the king wished to show his pleasure with him for having found Liall, though Gildar insisted that he deserved no credit for this since it was by chance that he had come on him.

Others, the king's captains and the ladies and men of the court, sat at the cross table and when wine was poured they raised their goblets to Liall, drinking his health and speaking of their joy at his safe return, for it was clear that he was much loved.

Food was served, and when they had eaten—Neva and Ivo rather lightly for the dishes seemed rich and strange to them—the king asked Liall for a full account of what had happened to him. This Liall did as best he could, explaining that though he knew Ivo had rescued him and Neva had cared for him, he could remember nothing else and that Neva and Ivo could not either.

"You do not know where they took you after you were wounded?"

"No, uncle."

"How can that be?" He turned to Ivo. "I know your names and that you are brother and sister. But beyond that, who are you?"

"Sire, we do not know."

"You do not know who your parents are?"

"No, sire. Liall does not remember what happened after he was struck down. We cannot remember anything at all—not even where we lived."

The king looked at him intently, then turned to the high steward.

"What think you of this, Zothar?"

"Sire, we know that what occurred took place near the Forest of Faraon, and we also know that parts of it are said to be enchanted. It is possible that a spell was put on them."

"Yes," said the king. Though he had been most courteous to Neva, his attention had been directed even more towards Ivo. Now he studied him again. "I will say two things. No matter who your folk are, they are not common folk. And though what you say is hard to credit, I believe you are telling the truth and know no more about yourselves than you say you do."

"Thank you, Your Majesty," said Ivo.

"Go on with your tale, Liall," said the king. "Do you know where you had been before you met Gildar?"

"Yes, uncle. We had crossed Morven and climbed Tarec in the Wendery Hills."

"You climbed Tarec?"

"Yes."

"Why? You must have known that it is forbidden, dangerous. But even if it were not, if you were well enough to travel, why did you not come home?"

Liall glanced at Neva and Ivo.

"Because a quest had been given to us."

"By whom?"

"We do not know."

"That is gone from your minds, too?"

"Yes. Though we all remembered what it was we

were to do, none of us remembered who had given it to us."

"And what was this quest?"

"To find a stone on Tarec: a stone that would tell us how to bring peace between Andor and Brunn."

The king became ominously still.

"And did you find the stone?"

"Yes, uncle. But it was broken. And though Neva and Ivo could read it, parts of it were missing so we could not understand what it said."

"That is well," said the king. Then suddenly and violently, "Peace! How can you talk of peace when those in Brunn are responsible—not just for the deaths of my wife and son—but of my brother, your father, too?"

"There have been deaths on their side, too, uncle. Their king, for instance. Besides, all that took place many years ago."

"And have there not been wanton and murderous assaults on us since then? Would they not have killed you if it had not been for your friends here?"

"That was just a border clash. They did not know who I was."

"And if they had known, do you not think they would have made even greater efforts to kill you?"

"No, uncle."

"I believe the prince is right, sire," said Zothar. "They treated the emissary you sent them with all due courtesy. And though you were sure they were lying when they said they were not holding him captive, we know now that they were speaking the truth."

"Yes, that was truly a marvel—for those in Brunn to speak the truth about anything! But this present state that is neither peace nor war has gone on long enough!"

"What do you mean by that, uncle?"

"That is no concern of yours. Let us talk of other things."

"But . . ."

"I said we will talk of other things!"

Liall met his eye for a moment, then bowed.

"Very well, uncle. How is my mother?"

"You have not seen her?"

"No, not yet. I thought I would go to her after we had talked."

"She is unchanged, so it makes little difference when you go. But you should go anyway."

"Yes, uncle," said Liall, rising. "Would you like to come with me?" he asked Neva and Ivo.

"If the king gives us leave," said Neva.

"Yes, yes," said the king. "It may help you to understand why I feel as I do about Brunn. We will talk again." And he held out his goblet so that his cupbearer could give him some more wine.

Neva and Ivo followed Liall out of the great hall, leaving the king brooding at the high table with Zothar watching him unhappily.

Liall led them back up the stairs and along the

corridor to a door at the end. Here he paused, looking at them strangely and uncertainly.

"Before we go in I think I should warn you not to be surprised at what will happen. My mother is not herself."

"She is ill?" asked Ivo.

"No. Though it could be called an illness of the mind or the spirit. For as you will see, she does not know me. She has known little and no one since the day word was brought to her, many years ago, that my father had been killed."

He knocked once, then opened the door and went in, followed by Neva and Ivo. They were in one of the tower rooms, large and circular, with many windows. In the centre of the room a woman with white hair sat at an embroidery frame, her needle flashing in the light of the tapers.

"Greetings, mother," said Liall.

She paused for a moment, looking up at him, and Neva and Ivo could see that though she was beautiful, her face still young and unlined, her eyes were deep-set and full of shadows.

"Who do you call mother?"

"Who but you, my lady?"

"I am no one's mother as I am no one's wife. I had a son once. And a husband. Now I have no one."

"You have me, mother," said Liall patiently. "I am your son."

"I know you. You have been here before, always

saying the same thing. But I do not know these others who are here with you. Who are they?"

"They are my very good friends, Neva and Ivo."

"They are not from Brunn?"

"No, mother."

"That is well." She looked at Neva. "The girl is lovely. Are you skilled at needlework, my dear?"

"No, my lady. I do not think I have ever done any."

"I could teach you. There is no one more skilled at it than I am. See?" She waved her hand and looking around they saw that the walls of the room were covered with tapestries, all exquisitely done in many colors. They were, however, all scenes of destruction: bloody battles, cities with their walls breached and their towers overthrown, and in all of them the victors bore the rampant bear of Andor on their banners and bucklers and the vanquished the sea serpent of Brunn.

"They are very beautiful, my lady," said Neva.

"Beautiful? Who cares if they are beautiful? All that matters is if they are potent. For there are curses worked into each of them."

And looking at them more closely, Neva and Ivo saw that, in addition to the many figures, each of them was embroidered with strange signs, the vertical lines barbed and stabbing downward like strokes of lightning.

"Well?" asked the white-haired lady. "Will you help me with my work?"

"I am not sure it is work I can do," said Neva. "But if I may, I will come and visit you."

"I do not need visitors. I need someone to help me. But only someone who feels as I do, hates as I do, can do that." And she went back to her needlework.

"It is getting late, mother," said Liall. "Shall I call your tiring women to prepare you for bed?"

But the white-haired lady did not answer, did not look at him, not even when he bent and kissed her. He straightened up, his eyes almost as dark and filled with pain as hers, and motioning to Neva and Ivo, he left the room.

Chapter 11

"Well?" said Liall.

"Has she been that way for a long time?" asked Neva.

"For as long as I can remember."

"It must be very difficult for you. I'm sorry."

Liall shrugged, but his face was still sombre. There were footsteps behind them, and Zothar came up the corridor towards them.

"How was she, Prince?" he asked.

"As my uncle said, the same."

Zothar nodded. "So I found her when I visited her at noon. Prince, I know that you have had a day of hard riding, but if you are not too tired I would like to talk to you."

"I am not too tired."

"Then will you and your friends come to my chamber with me?"

Liall glanced at Neva and Ivo and when they nodded, he said, "Of course." And they followed the steward up a narrow stair and into a room above the one they had just left. It, too, was round with many windows, but its walls were bare, and it was much more simply furnished. There was a long table between two of the windows with an ink pot, quill pen and many parchment scrolls on it.

"It has been some time since I was last here," said Liall looking around.

"You used to come quite often when you were younger. But as you can see, it has not changed." Zothar pulled out stools for all of them and sat down himself. "I wanted to talk to you about the king. I think you know what he is planning."

"War with Brunn?"

"Yes. I thought you had guessed it."

"I did not have to guess. When we met Gildar he told us he had been in Westfell, raising a levy of horsemen."

"I see. You have made clear how you feel about that, and I think you know how I do. But it may be that your friends do not know."

"You are against it?" said Neva.

"Yes, my lady. I have been ever since I took over the stewardship. At that time the king was much more reasonable, and it was I who suggested a plan to him that I thought would ensure a lasting peace between Andor and Brunn."

"I know something about that but there is much I do not know," said Liall. "There was to be an exchange of hostages, was there not?"

"Yes," said Zothar. "The king's son, Halidar, was then little more than a year old. And though the queen was greatly opposed to it, he agreed to send the boy to Brunn if King Brennir would send his daughter here. The exchange was to take place at the border, but something went wrong. A battle broke out and Halidar was killed."

"What went wrong?" asked Ivo.

"No one is certain—not even I who was there. The king insists that it was a betrayal—an attempt to capture Prince Halidar. But in any case many were slain, including, it is said, the Princess Varena of Brunn. And so my attempt to find peace made things worse than they had ever been. For open, bloody war followed in which again many fell."

"My father," said Liall.

"Yes. And King Brennir who was leading the hosts of Brunn. But the evil and sorrow did not stop at the battlefield. For your aunt, Queen Narda, whom the king loved dearly, died of grief when she learned that her son had been lost. And you know what happened to your mother."

Liall nodded.

"But as Liall said before, that was many years ago," said Neva. "Why is the king preparing for war again now?"

"He has never forgiven Brunn, as Liall's mother has not," said Zothar. "And when he thought Liall was killed or captured, all the old wounds were opened again. Besides, he is getting on in years and he is determined to destroy Brunn while he is still able to take the field himself."

"And can nothing be done to stop him?" asked Ivo.

"I will go on trying to do so, as I have been doing. But there is small chance that I will succeed. Our best hope, it seems, lies elsewhere."

"Where?" asked Liall.

"In the word you brought. You truly do not know who gave you the quest you talked of, or told you about the stone on Tarec?"

"No," said Liall, and both Neva and Ivo shook their heads.

Zothar studied them each in turn, looking deep into their eyes.

"I believe you," he said finally. "But then it must be that some power has decided to intervene and is using you as its instrument."

"You have always been interested in ancient lore," said Liall. "What power could that be?"

"I don't know," said Zothar. "There are many powers in the land, both good and evil."

"You think this one could be evil?" asked Neva.

"Since it is clearly on our side, no. And while I do not believe I can do anything with the king, I still may be able to do something. You said you could read the stone you found on Tarec?"

"Not all of it," said Neva. "Some parts of it were missing."

"And what did it say?"

Neva hesitated for a moment, then told him. Zothar looked thoughtful, then went to a small chest near the table and took out a small, flat fragment of black stone.

"Could this be one of the pieces that were missing?"

"Yes!" said Ivo. "That's the piece the gore-crow flew off with. Liall was going to ask you about it."

"You knew I had it?"

"Yes."

"How?"

Ivo told him about Akala and what he had reported to them.

"This is all very strange," said Zothar. "I thought so when the crow dropped the stone—that is why I kept it. Now I am glad I did. Here." And he gave the fragment of stone to Neva.

"We will need a looking glass to read it," she said.

Zothar raised a surprised eyebrow at this, but he did not ask why. He got a polished metal mirror from a cupboard and handed it to her. She held the stone fragment in front of it, and she and Ivo looked at its reflection.

"There's just one word on it," said Ivo. " 'Daughter.' "

"No," said Neva, pointing to a short slanting line on the edge of the fragment. "This stroke here is a possessive. If this piece fits where I think it does the inscription reads, 'Arnor and Brunn shall again be one when Ima's daughter marries . . .' and then there's another piece missing."

"That was something else we meant to ask you about," said Liall. "Who is Ima?"

"Those in Brunn claim that she was a goddess," said Zothar, "though she was probably one of their first queens. In any case, she is revered there as the founder of Brunn, as we revere Kennar as our first ancestor."

"But she must have lived centuries ago," said Liall. "How could she have a daughter who could still marry?"

"I don't know," said Zothar. "If we could find the last fragment of stone—the part that is still missing—that might become clear."

"How can we find it?" asked Ivo. "It is a wonder almost beyond belief that we should have found this one."

"Still it did come into our hands," said Zothar. "Which I take to be a sign that some power is on our side. And we have need of such help, for there is little time left. And if the king does attack Brunn, as he intends to do, that will be the end of all hope of peace forever."

"Forever?" said Liall. "We want war no more than you do. But Andor and Brunn have fought many times before this. And afterwards there was always quiet for some years if not true peace."

"That is so. But this time it is different."

"Different how?" asked Neva.

Zothar looked at them gravely for a moment.

"Since the king knows that I do not hold with him in this, he no longer trusts me and has not told me when he intends to strike. But you have trusted me, telling me all that you know, and so I will tell you."

Taking a key from his pouch, he unlocked a cupboard and brought out a large hour-glass and set it on the table. The sand in it was black, and very little of it remained in the top portion.

"My father, who was steward before me, gave me this when he knew he was about to die, instructing me to show it to no one unless the need was great. He said he was forbidden to say where he had gotten it, but that it should serve as both a spur to me and a guide in all my counsels. For it measured, not only time, but the very life of Andor."

"What do you mean?" asked Liall.

"He said—and he never spoke lightly—that if there was not true peace between Andor and Brunn before the sands ran out, then that would be the end for us and for them. For there would never be peace."

They all stared at the glass, watching as the sand sifted down almost, it seemed, a grain at a time.

"How much time is left?" asked Neva.

"As you can see, very little. I would say not more than a fortnight and perhaps less."

"I do not know what more we can do," said Liall.

"Nor do I," said Zothar. "But our talk has heartened me and made me more hopeful than I have been in many years. Let us all think about it and talk again. In the meantime, it is late and I have kept you too long from your beds."

"I am weary," said Liall. And with a last glance at the hour-glass, they said good night to Zothar and went out and down the stairs to their own chambers.

Chapter 12

"You slept late this morning," said the king. "Much later than is your custom. I trust you slept well."

"I did, uncle," said Liall.

"And your friends?"

"We slept very well, Your Majesty," said Ivo.

"I'm glad," said the king. "By your account you travelled far and did much and had need of rest. But what do you plan to do today?"

They were standing outside the great hall where they had broken their fast and when they were leaving it they had come upon the king.

"We thought we would go hawking," said Liall.

"So I suspected," said the king, looking at Neva who had on a riding dress. "Are you good falconers?"

"I don't know, sire," she said. "I'm not sure that Ivo and I have ever done it before."

"That is another thing you can't remember?"

"Yes, sire."

"Perhaps it will come back to you when you try it." Then turning to Ivo, "I see that you're wearing a sword as you did when you arrived here. Can you use it?"

"Yes, sire. At least I think so."

"He can," said Liall. "And very well."

"How do you know?"

"Because I saw him fight a Hilti out in the Morven."

"And who taught you to use it?" the king asked Ivo.

"I don't know, sire. But I have the feeling that I was well trained."

His eyes on him, the king nodded, and Ivo suddenly realized that his questions had been far from idle; that he was testing their whole story with them, searching for inconsistencies. And the king must have sensed that he had guessed this for he said, "You must forgive me, but everything you have told me is very strange."

"It cannot seem stranger to you than it does to us, sire," said Ivo. "But it is the truth."

"I believe you. And where will you go hawking?"

"We'll start in the river meadows," said Liall. "And if we raise nothing there, we'll try the heath."

"If you do go to the heath, stay on the near side of it," said the king. "Don't go too far north."

"Why not?" asked Liall.

"Because I don't wish you to," said the king, frowning.

"Is that a warning, uncle?" asked Liall, his lips tightening.

"Yes," said the king. "Haven't we all suffered enough at the hands of those from Brunn? If you go near the border, you'll be stopped!"

He and Liall looked at one another, and it was clear that Liall was angry and resentful. But while Ivo could understand this, he knew that the king had been sorely tried and now felt himself opposed—not only by his chief adviser, the high steward—but by his closest kin, his own nephew. And looking at his strong, lined face Ivo felt—not only sympathetic—but drawn to him.

The king saw this, and his face softened.

"Your friend understands me better than you do, Liall. I am no tyrant, but I will not have my plans interfered with. Good hunting." And he strode off.

"Shall we still go?" asked Neva.

"Of course," said Liall shortly, and he led the way to the palace courtyard and across it to the mews.

When Ivo had awakened that morning, it had taken him a moment to remember where he was. Then it had all come flooding back, not only their arrival at Lantar and their meeting with the king, but their later one with Zothar. He felt the old familiar sense of loss when he realized that was all he remembered. Though they now knew a little more of what the inscription said, the spell was still on him. At the same time this small new bit of knowledge, along with what Zothar had told them, made their quest more urgent than ever. Dressing quickly, he had knocked at the door of Neva's room and had barely greeted her when Liall had joined them. They had agreed that they must talk and also decided that it would be better not to do so in the palace where they could be overheard.

"Where shall we go then?" Neva had asked.

"We shall go hawking," Liall had said. "That is one way we can be alone." And he had gone off to borrow a riding dress for her from one of the ladies who attended his mother.

Iskan, the king's falconer, was sitting on a bench outside the mews and braiding a new jess for one of the hawks. An elderly man, his face lined and leathery, he rose and greeted Liall warmly, for they were old friends. He went into the mews with them, took one of the peregrine falcons from her perch, hooded her and gave her to Liall. Then, as they were about to leave, he said, "I hear you were in the far west and climbed Tarec."

"Yes," said Liall. "Where did you hear it?"

"Oh, word gets about. I was there myself many years ago, about the time you were born."

"And climbed Tarec also?"

"Yes."

"It is a difficult climb."

"Not so difficult. I come from Dernan where there are much higher peaks. Afterwards I heard that it was a forbidden mountain, but I did not know that then and I saw nothing of the watcher of whom many speak."

"What of the black stone that was set there? Did you see that?"

"I did. In fact I was there the day it was shattered."

Liall stiffened. "The day? . . ."

"Yes."

"How did that happen?"

"At that time your uncle was a great falconer, and I had gone there to get an eaglet for him. There are many eyries in those parts."

"Yes," said Liall. "You went alone?"

"I started out alone," said Iskan, "crossing the marshes and going up into the hills from the south. But when I climbed Tarec I had a companion; the falconer of King Brennir of Brunn."

"That seems odd—for you to have a companion from Brunn."

"Not so odd. Things were not so bad then. There was even talk of peace between Andor and Brunn. But even if there hadn't been, it would not have mattered for, as you know, there is a bond between falconers that recognizes no boundaries."

"That's true. He was a friend of yours, the falconer from Brunn?"

"Not to begin with. His name was Largar, and we met for the first time near the foot of Tarec. He was there for the same reason I was—to take an eaglet if he could. So we climbed the mountain together."

"And you were there when the stone was shattered?" asked Neva.

"Yes, my lady, though we did not see it happen. We had been on the peak, seen the stone and had talked about it. Largar said it had been set there by the goddess who founded Brunn."

"Ima," said Liall.

"Yes. Well, we had just started down towards an eyrie we had spied when there was a bright flash of light and a great crash behind us."

"What had caused it?" asked Ivo.

"We were not sure. It looked and sounded like a lightning bolt, though the sky was clear. In any case, we went back up, and there was the stone, shattered, split and lying on its face."

"That's the way we found it," said Liall. "It's strange that you should have been there when it happened."

"It was strange. Largar was very disturbed by it. He said it was an omen that boded ill for Brunn and perhaps for Andor, too. And he picked up a piece of the stone to take back to Brunn with him."

"He what?" said Liall.

"Picked up a piece of the stone to show to King Brennir."

"Was there writing on it—the piece he took?" asked Neva.

"There was something on it that may have been writing, but we could not read it."

"And he took it back to Brunn with him?" Liall asked.

"Yes, Prince. I never saw him again but I have often thought of him. He was older than I was and a great falconer. I learned much from him in the short time we were together."

"As I learned much from you, Iskan," said Liall.

"Well, you always had a feeling for the hawks, Prince," said Iskan, smiling. "But I did not mean to keep you here for so long telling you of things that happened long ago. I hope the peregrine flies well."

Liall thanked him, and they left the mews.

"Wait," he said as Ivo started to say something. "We have more to talk about now than ever. But let us do it later."

So Ivo restrained himself while they went around behind the mews to the stables. A groom brought out horses for them, and they mounted and with the falcon on Liall's fist rode across the square and out through the town gates.

"Well?" said Liall when they were in the meadows near the river.

"When Zothar showed us the fragment of stone

last night, he said he took it to be a sign that some power was on our side, guiding us," said Ivo. "If I doubted it then, I do no longer. For here, beyond all expectation, we have been told where the last piece is."

"I agree," said Liall. "The question is what we should do about it. What say you, Neva?"

"I think it is you who should say. For while the quest was given to all of us—and if you are right our fate is greatly involved in it—still your case is different from ours."

"How so?"

"Though there is nothing that Ivo and I want more than to have the spell that is on us lifted, that is a matter that concerns only the two of us. You, on the other hand, have responsibilities and allegiances that we do not."

"You mean not only to Andor but to my uncle."

"Yes."

"But what if I think that my uncle is wrong?"

Neither Neva nor Ivo answered.

"Well, that is what I do think," said Liall. "I think that what Andor needs is peace, not war. And even if that were not the issue, I would be a poor friend if I were not as anxious to see you returned to yourselves as you are. And so I think we should go to Brunn and see if we can find the last fragment of the stone."

Ivo relaxed. From the time Iskan had told them his

story he had determined that he and Neva would go to Brunn even if Liall did not.

"I'm glad, Liall," he said. "But it may not be easy to go. You heard what the king said."

"I heard. And I do not think it will be easy. But if we are meant to go—as I think we are—it may be that we shall be helped there, too. So shall we ride?"

Neva and Ivo exchanged glances and both smiled at him. Then, turning their horses, they rode north away from the river and towards the heath.

It was almost noon when they had talked to Iskan and by the time they had left the meadows, farms and fields behind them and were on the heath the sun was well on its way to the west. They paused on top of a rise and looked about them. Some sheep grazed nearby; an old ram watching them curiously. Far to the north they could see the green line of the forest that separated Andor and Brunn. But apart from the sheep nothing else moved on the vast rolling expanse of the heath.

This was as far as they had been told they could go and as Liall sent his horse forward again, Ivo said, "Should we not at least pretend that we are hawking?"

"Who is to see if we are or not?" asked Liall and they rode on.

When they were at the bottom of the rise, Neva turned, looking behind her and said, "Look!"

They turned also. Flying towards them from the south was a dark bird. As it drew nearer, it came lower and soon they could see that it was a gore-crow—and none of them doubted that it was the one that had flown off with the fragment of stone on Tarec.

It circled overhead once, so low that they could see the sheen of its feathers and the gleam of its eye as it looked down at them, then it flew off again the way it had come, back towards Lantar.

"Perhaps we should do some hawking after all," said Liall grimly, and unhooding the falcon, he cast her off into the wind.

Though unprepared, she was away at once, her great pointed wings taking her upward to gain her pitch. When she was well above them, she saw the crow and swinging around in a tight arc, she stooped, closing her wings and diving down on it with her sharp claws forward and ready. The crow flapped on, apparently unaware of the feathered death that was coming down on it. But as the falcon was about to strike, the crow veered and rose to meet it. The two birds were too far away and too high for any of them to see what happened, but when they separated it was the falcon that was falling while the crow flew on, disappearing behind the high ground to the south.

The falcon struck the ground and lay still. Liall rode towards her, and Neva and Ivo followed.

"This I have never seen nor heard of," said Liall, looking down at the lifeless body. "That a crow should kill a falcon."

"If there is a power that is on our side, helping us,"

said Neva, "why should there not also be one that is against us? It was not by chance that the stone was shattered. It was broken so that it could not be read. And that must also be why the monster was there, guarding it."

"From the time I first saw the crow, I did not think it was an ordinary one," said Liall.

"And now it has gone off to tell someone where we are and what we are about," said Ivo. "Do we still go on?"

"Yes," said Liall firmly. "Without pretense now, and as quickly as we can." And he put his horse into a canter.

They were still some eight or ten miles from the border, and they rode steadily, never pressing their horses but never slackening their pace. When they drew closer to the forest, they saw a break in it somewhat to the west and recognized the Burnt Place that they had passed on their way to Morven.

"There?" asked Ivo.

"It will be easier to cross there than finding our way through the forest," said Liall.

But as they turned towards it, they heard a shrill horn blast and, coming over a hill to their left, they saw a dozen or more armed riders.

"This is what the king meant," said Neva, reining in. "What now?"

"They are our men and will know me," said Liall. "It may be that I can talk to them."

"Even if they don't have their orders—and they must have—they will never let you go over into Brunn," said Ivo.

"Are you saying we should give up then?"

"No. But we have need of some sleight or trick to do what we wish. Let us ride towards them slowly. Then we'll turn and try for the forest."

Liall measured the distance to the advancing patrol.

"It may be that we can do it," he said. "Let us try."

They started forward again, walking their horses and edging closer to the forest as they approached the patrol. Seeing them coming towards them, the border guards slowed up also, and their captain waved to them. Liall waved back. Then,

"Now!" said Ivo and pulling his horse around sharply, he put it into a gallop, riding straight for the forest.

He heard a shout behind him and, looking back, saw that the guards were galloping after them. It was going to be close.

They were some forty or fifty yards from the forest now, and he scanned it, looking for a place where the trees grew far enough apart for them to ride through. He saw such a place between an oak and a beech, and he rode towards it, but just before he reached it, his horse swerved away and reared, whinnying in fear, and almost threw him. With an exclamation, he tried to turn it back and try again, but he could not. Out of the corner of his eye he saw that

Neva's and Liall's horses had balked also.

"Here," said a voice. "Quickly!"

About ten paces to their right, standing half in the forest and half out as if he were holding open a door, was a tall, grey-bearded man.

Neva, who was closest to him, rode towards him, and Ivo and Liall followed. Catching Neva's horse by the bridle, the grey-bearded man led it into the forest, then stood aside while Ivo and Liall went in after her. Behind them they could hear the pounding of hoofs as the patrol galloped up, then shouts and whinnies as the horses reared and balked as their own had done. Scowling angrily, the captain was fighting his mount, trying again and again to get it to enter the forest. But somehow Ivo knew that he would not be able to. The door, if it had been a door, was closed.

Chapter 13

"You are safe now," said the grey-bearded man. "They will not come in here."

"Then the tales that are told about the forest are true," said Neva.

"I do not know what tales you mean," said the man. "But none can come in without leave."

"Your leave?" asked Liall.

"In this case, yes."

He was tall—a little taller than Ivo—and powerfully built. His features were craggy and though his hair and beard were grey his blue eyes were sharp and clear.

"Why did you let us in?" asked Ivo.

"Because you seemed to need help."

"We did," said Ivo. "And we thank you for it. May we know your name?"

"Jartan."

"Mine is Ivo. And this is Neva and Liall."

He bowed slightly in acknowledgement. "Why were the guards chasing you?" he asked.

"To keep us from the border. We want to cross over into Brunn."

"Ah, yes. They are very strict about that."

"Could you help us there, too?" asked Liall. "Guide us through the forest?"

"Yes," said Jartan. "But you have been riding hard and your horses are tired. It might be best for you to spend the night here with me, and I will take you where you want to go in the morning."

"You're very kind," said Neva. "We would be most grateful."

He nodded gravely. "I will show you where you can leave your horses."

He picked up an axe that was lying nearby and set off along a narrow path.

"Are you a woodcutter?" asked Ivo.

"Among other things. Today I happened to be cutting wood."

They followed him, leading the horses. The trees were very tall and green and seemed strangely alive, bending and rustling softly though there was no wind. Finally they came to a large, grassy clearing where a grey charger was grazing. He raised his head when they appeared, stood at gaze for a moment and then neighed and their horses nickered in answer. The charger walked towards them as they unsaddled their horses, and when they turned them loose he rubbed noses with each in turn.

"He seems glad to see them," said Liall.

"Well, they're company," said Jartan. "There have been no other horses here for many years."

"Is he yours?" asked Ivo.

"He came here with me."

"Then he is yours."

"Is he? Can any living creature belong to anyone else?"

"I had not thought of that," said Ivo. "No."

Jartan stroked the grey charger's neck, then led the way back into the forest. This path was wider and they walked beside him rather than behind him. Suddenly a fox appeared out of the underbrush ahead of them. It stopped dead when it saw them and looked at them with wide brown eyes.

"It does not seem afraid," said Liall.

"Why should it be afraid?" said Jartan. "There is no hunting here nor killing of any kind."

"Is that by your commandment, too?"

"Nothing here is by my commandment."

"Whose then?"

"I cannot tell you that," said Jartan.

He looked fixedly at the fox, and the fox looked

back at him then, with some reluctance, went trotting off.

They continued on along the path and in a while came to another, smaller clearing with a hut in the center of it. Its wattle and daub walls were covered with ivy, it had a thatched roof, and there was a bench in front of the door.

"Strange," said Ivo. "I knew it would look like that."

"Do you come from these parts?" asked Jartan.

"We do not know."

"How is that?"

"We think a spell was put on us. In any case, we do not remember where we came from."

"There are such spells," said Jartan. "On the other hand, forest huts all look very much alike." He opened the door of the hut. "Are you hungry?"

They all realized suddenly that they had eaten nothing since late that morning.

"Yes," said Ivo.

"If you will wait out here, I will prepare our supper."

"May we walk about until then?" asked Liall.

"You may go where you like, do what you like."

He went into the hut, and they strolled across the clearing. There was another path on the far side of it, which they followed, walking under the whispering trees until they came to a large, clear forest pool. The sun was slanting down now, and though it was still pleasantly warm, the light was getting dim. Neva paused, staring across the pond and following her glance, Ivo saw two dark shapes there; a she bear and her cub, drinking.

They raised their heads and, seeing them, the cub squealed and started around the pond towards them. The she bear growled softly, and the cub hesitated, then went back to her and they disappeared into the trees.

"None of the animals seem to fear us, yet they all avoid us," said Liall.

"Yes," said Ivo. He glanced at Neva. "You've been very quiet since we came into the forest."

"I've been thinking."

"About what?"

She shrugged and he looked at her searchingly. "You feel that all this is familiar, too?"

"Yes. I knew what the hut would look like just as you did."

"That means nothing," said Liall. "As Jartan said, all forest huts look much alike."

"Perhaps," said Neva. "But did you notice his clothes?"

Ivo thought for a moment. "His tunic was like the ones we were wearing when we found ourselves out on the heath—made of the same silvery cloth."

"That means nothing either," said Liall. "It could just be the kind of cloth they weave in these parts."

"It could," said Neva. "And it could be more than that."

"You think that this is where we came from?" asked Ivo.

"Isn't it possible?"

"I suppose so. But then . . . Are you saying that Jartan is our father?"

Neva hesitated. "No. Somehow I don't think he is."

"Neither do I. If he were, I'm sure we'd know him, spell or no spell. And if he knew us, wouldn't he say so?"

"Perhaps there's a spell on him, too, so that he doesn't remember us any more than we do him."

"We could ask him about it."

"I don't think we should."

"Why not?"

"Because if Zothar was right and some power is helping us, then there's a reason for everything that has happened. And while we may wonder about things, I don't think we should inquire into them."

"You mean, if we were meant to know, we would know or would be told."

"Yes."

Ivo frowned. "Very well. Then we'll say nothing about it."

Though the path continued on around the pool, they went no farther but turned and walked back. When they reached the clearing, Jartan was waiting for them. He brought out bread and bowls of soup and they sat on the bench outside the hut and ate. The soup was thick, made of mushrooms and barley, and was very good. While they were eating, Ivo studied Jartan. He had an unusual face. There was strength in it and dignity, but also great kindness and warmth. Could he have seen it before—not once but many times—and still not be able to remember it? Jartan caught his glance and returned it openly and directly, and Ivo dropped his eyes.

When they could eat no more, Jartan said, "None from Andor cross over into Brunn without a good reason. Do you have such a reason?"

"We think we have," said Neva.

"Can you tell me what it is?"

"Yes. We hope that by doing so we can make peace between Andor and Brunn."

"That is indeed a good reason," said Jartan. "But it will not be easy. How do you hope to do it?"

"We're not sure," said Ivo. "There's something we hope to find there. If we do find it, it may give us the answer."

"It will not be easy even to enter Brunn. Guards watch the border there as they do in Andor. What will you tell them if they stop you and ask you who you are and where you come from?"

"We don't know," said Ivo. "What should we tell them?"

"You must come from somewhere in Brunn, but

from a place that is not too near lest they ask you questions about it that you cannot answer. Perhaps you should say you come from Nordan."

"Nordan?"

"It is far to the east and inland, high in the mountains."

"And what are we doing in these parts?" asked Liall.

"We must think of a reason," said Jartan. "Where do you wish to go in Brunn?"

"We don't know that either," said Liall. "But we should probably begin at Mirana."

Jartan nodded. "Their great trial-at-arms is to be held soon—I think tomorrow. You can say you're going to that."

"And what is this trial-at-arms?" asked Ivo.

"Once a year those who consider themselves skilled swordsmen gather at Mirana to compete in single combat. Count Jeranus, their war leader, and Tarnir, captain of the Queen's Guard, are the judges and they pick the best of the swordsmen to serve in the guard."

Neva's eyes became large and anxious.

"Are you saying that Ivo and Liall should enter the contest?" she said.

"No," said Jartan. "They can be going there merely to watch the swordplay. There is no need for them to take part in it."

"But can anyone who wishes do so?" asked Ivo.

"Yes. But why do you ask?"

"It is just something I thought we should know."

"I take it that you are something of a swordsman?"

"He is," said Liall. "The best that I've seen."

"It's possible that you would do well in the contests," said Jartan. "Even well enough to be chosen as one of the queen's guards. But what purpose would that serve?"

"It would give us a reason for staying on in Mirana," said Ivo.

"And you think that is necessary?"

"It might be."

"Well, that is for you to decide. But there is one other thing. Your name and Neva's would mean nothing in Brunn. But yours, Liall, is almost as well known there as it is in Andor."

"You know who I am then?" asked Liall.

"Yes. And I would call myself something else if I were you."

"What would you call yourself?"

"Since you will be saying that you are from Nordan, you could call yourself Nord."

"Nord of Nordan," said Liall. "Very well."

Jartan took the bowls into the hut, and Neva looked at Ivo.

"You *are* thinking of going into the trial-at-arms, aren't you?" she said.

"I'm not sure."

"Aren't you? I think you are!" she said bitterly and

getting up she walked off into the forest.

"Why is she so angry?" asked Ivo.

"Surely you know," said Liall. "It could be dangerous, and she is your sister and very fond of you."

"Yes," said Ivo.

It was dark when Neva came back. She said nothing to either of them, and they all went into the hut. Jartan showed them where they should sleep: Neva in a room by herself, and Ivo and Liall in another one. Jartan himself slept in an alcove near the fireplace in the large room.

Tired from their long ride, Ivo fell asleep almost at once but woke sometime in the middle of the night and lay there for a while listening to Liall's breathing and the soft sighing of the leaves outside. He felt strange, different, and at first he could not tell why. Then it came to him. For days now—the short time that he could remember—he had been living with a deep and frightening sense of loss. For as Neva had said in a different way, how could a man say, "I am," if he did not know who he was? He had done those things which needed to be done but always with a feeling of uncertainty as if the very ground he walked on might give way, vanish as the past that had shaped him had. And whenever he had tried to go back, think back, he had been checked as his horse had been when he had tried to enter the forest. But he was in the forest now. Jartan had let him in. And though their quest would now take them into a place that was alien, unknown, and where the slightest mistake could be disastrous, he was not anxious. For the first time since he had found himself walking on the heath with Neva and Liall, he did not feel lost. It was as if he had come home after a long journey. And, at that moment at least, he felt—not only at peace—but hopeful, able to believe that if their quest was successful he would find that which he had been seeking—himself.

Though they were up early the next morning, Jartan was up before them. He had baked oat cakes, and after they had eaten, he went to the large clearing with them. Their horses were rested and stood quietly while they were saddled, but seemed curiously unwilling to leave the pasture. It was only after the grey charger had nuzzled each of them that Neva was able to lead hers to where Jartan waited and the others followed.

Jartan led them north through the forest. He did not seem to be following a track or trail but he never hesitated, walking steadily ahead of them around fallen trees and patches of briars and waiting for them when they fell behind. Finally, about midmorning, he paused in a copse of beech trees and said, "There is Brunn."

On the far side of the trees was a grassy plain that stretched green and level to the distant horizon.

"We thank you for your help and your hospitality," said Neva.

He nodded and gave her a packet wrapped in green leaves.

"There is food in there," he said. "You may need it before you get to Mirana."

"We thank you for that, too," said Ivo.

"There is naught to thank me for. But I must still let you out."

Going to the edge of the copse, he raised his hands, pressing outward, then turned sideways, leaning back as if holding a door ajar.

"I wish you well on your quest. Be wary and discreet, but also of good heart for there is more in your favor than you know."

"That we have long suspected," said Ivo. "Will we see you again?"

"It may well be. When you are ready to come back, come this way. It will always be a place of refuge for you. And now, farewell."

"Farewell, Jartan," said Ivo. Stepping forward impulsively, he embraced him. Then, mounting, he rode out of the forest and onto the plain. Neva and Liall went after him. When they turned and looked back the green wall of the trees was unbroken and there was no sign of Jartan.

Chapter 14

Though they were uncertain about the exact location of Mirana, they knew it was on the sea, so they rode north, sure that sooner or later they would meet someone who would direct them to it. When they had gone about a mile from the forest, they spied horsemen in the distance, coming from the west, and they rode towards them. As they approached, they saw that it was a patrol of a dozen men, all bearing bucklers with the sea-serpent of Brunn on them.

Their leader, a sturdy man whose close-cropped hair was just touched with grey, nodded to them as they drew rein.

"Greetings," he said. "Who are you and from whence do you come?"

"We are from Nordan," said Liall. "My name is Nord. This is my friend, Ivo, and his sister, Neva."

"And where are you going?"

"To Mirana for the trial-at-arms."

The youngest member of the patrol, a rangy, red-headed trooper who had been staring at Neva, laughed shortly.

"Nordan is known for its wool and its goat cheese," he said. "But who ever heard of a swordsman who came from there?"

"Because you never heard of any, that does not mean that there are none," said Liall coldly.

"You?"

"That's enough, Vassek," said the patrol leader. And turning back to Liall, "Then you are entering the trial-at-arms?"

"I doubt it," said Liall. "But we thought we would like to see the contests."

"They are well worth seeing," said Vassek. "And will be more so than ever this year."

"You can ride with us," said the patrol leader. "We are on our way to Mirana."

"Thank you," said Liall somewhat stiffly.

The patrol leader shook his horse into a canter, and they set off together, riding north across the plain.

"Your friend is touchy," said the patrol leader to Ivo, who was riding beside him.

"Yes, he is," said Ivo.

"He should not mind Vassek. As you may have

guessed, he is entering the trial-at-arms. He is a very good swordsman, the best in the patrol and probably the best of any who ride the border."

"And it appears that he knows it."

"Well, he is young and pleased with himself. By the way, my name is Brock."

"You already know mine," said Ivo.

He glanced back. Neva was riding behind them, with Liall on one side of her and Vassek on the other. Vassek was leaning towards her, talking earnestly, and it was clear from her expression that she did not like whatever it was he was saying and neither did Liall, for he was looking angrily at the red-headed trooper and shifting in his saddle.

"Excuse me," said Ivo to Brock.

Pulling up his horse, he circled around, came up behind Vassek and pushed in between him and Neva, jostling Vassek as he did and throwing his mount off-stride so that it stumbled.

"Whoa there!" said Vassek, steadying his horse. "What are you up to?"

"I would like to talk to my sister."

"We don't expect much of anyone from Nordan, but I would have thought they would teach you some manners!"

"I would have thought the same of one from Mirana."

"You're talking about me?" said Vassek, scowling.

"Who else?"

"That will do, Vassek," said Brock, circling around also. "Fall back."

"What?"

"I said fall back!"

Vassek hesitated, glaring at Brock as well as at Ivo, then dropped back and took his place at the end of the column.

"Thank you, Ivo," said Neva as they went on again.

"Why are you thanking me? I don't like our red-headed friend, and I didn't think you did either."

"No. He was telling me how well he was going to do at the trial-at-arms. That he was sure to be picked for the Queen's Guard and suggesting that I go to a tavern with him afterwards to celebrate."

"I thought it was something like that."

They rode on, cantering steadily across the grassy plain. By late morning they were riding through farmland, and shortly after that, they saw Mirana in the distance. It was a large town, even larger than Lantar, built on the edge of a cliff, and beyond it they could catch glimpses of the sea. Shortly before noon they came to a field just outside the town gates. There were tents and booths set around it, and at its centre, opposite a pavilion, was an open space surrounded by a low fence of woven willow.

The field was crowded with people—men, women and children in holiday dress, men-at-arms in steel caps and byrnies and sailors in baggy white breeches and brightly colored shirts—walking between the booths, standing in front of them and eating the broiled meat and fish that was being cooked there or sitting on the closely cut grass.

Brock led them to a paddock where they dismounted and tethered their horses. They thanked him for having let them ride with him and, taking the food that Jartan had given them, they left the paddock and began looking for a place where they could eat.

There was a fountain at the edge of the field, and they sat on its coping and ate the flat bread, cheese and dried fruit that they had found in Jartan's packet.

They had just finished when there was a trumpet blast and the crowd began moving towards the enclosure in the centre of the field. By the time they reached it, the crowd was thick about the fenced-in area, but Brock, standing in the front row, called to them and those near him let them through so they could join him.

Two ladies now sat on cushioned chairs in the pavilion with three men standing behind them. Even without her crown and embroidered purple gown, the older of the women would have looked regal. There was authority in her stillness and the way she held herself, but pain had lined her face prematurely and a deep sadness made her blue eyes seem darker than they were. The other, sitting beside her, was young, her long hair black as a midnight sky, its gloss like the shining of summer stars. And though she sat as quietly as her companion, there was such animation in her face and wide-set eyes that she seemed almost restless.

"Is that the queen?" asked Neva.

"Yes," said Brock. "And her niece, the Princess Devita."

"They're wonderful looking," said Neva. "The queen is beautiful."

"So is the princess," said Ivo.

"Who are the men?" asked Liall.

"The tallest of them, the grey-haired man in the cloak, is Count Jeranus, our war leader. The man next to him is Tarnir, Captain of the Queen's guard. They are the judges in the trial-at-arms."

"And the bearded man in the dark robe?"

"The queen's brother, Cadorno, Warden of Brunn."

Jeranus and Tarnir had been conferring, and now Tarnir stepped forward.

"We have a new entrant in the trials," he announced. "And since he has just arrived from the border with his patrol, we have agreed to let him meet the winner of this morning's matches."

"That will be Vassek," said Brock.

There was a scattering of applause, and Vassek swaggered into the enclosure where he was joined by a light-haired youth with a somewhat shy smile.

"Who is he?" asked Ivo.

"His name is Dannus," said Brock. "This is the

first time he has fought in the trials, but his father was in the Queen's Guard and he is said to be a very good swordsman."

Vassek and Dannus saluted the queen and princess, then faced one another and at a signal from Tarnir began their match.

Dannus was good—nimble and quick in his responses—but it was soon clear that Vassek was even better. He was not only stronger, but much more aggressive. He wasted no time in feeling Dannus out but began an immediate attack, pressing him hard. Dannus fell back, defending himself skillfully, but Vassek gave him no chance to do anything but parry, driving him into a corner of the enclosure. Then, when he had him penned there, he pressed him even harder, cutting at him with wide-swinging horseman's blows. One of these, glancing off Dannus' buckler, slashed his arm. He grimaced with pain, and before he could recover, Vassek struck again, knocking the sword from his grasp and then running him through the shoulder.

Neva gasped as Dannus sank to his knees.

"Did Vassek have to do that?" she asked.

"No," said Brock. "Once he had disarmed Dannus the match was over."

Though both Tarnir and Jeranus were frowning, evidently feeling as Brock did about that last, unnecessary wound, the crowd roared its approval and Vassek stepped back, nodding and smiling.

At a gesture from Tarnir, two guards entered the enclosure, helped Dannus to his feet and led him away to the healer's tent.

"Will he be all right?" asked Neva.

"Yes," said Brock. "Though it will be some time before he can use that arm again."

Now Tarnir stepped forward.

"Before we declare Vassek the winner at this year's trial-at-arms is there anyone present who wishes to challenge him?"

He waited, looking around, and so did Vassek, still smiling in triumph.

"It does not seem right that I should be called the winner after only one match," he said with mock modesty. "Is there no one who will try even a few hand-strokes with me?" His eyes were on Neva now. He was staring at her openly and boldly, seeking her approval, and when she looked back at him coldly, he frowned and his eyes went to Ivo. "What about our visitors from Nordan? Or was your talk about swordsmen from there just talk and do you carry swords merely to cut cheese with?"

Ivo flushed, angered not so much by what he said as by the way he had been looking at Neva.

"No, it was not merely talk," he said. "I challenge you."

There was a stir and murmur from the crowd, and all those who stood nearby turned and looked at him. Vassek stiffened, frowning in surprise.

"Are you mad, Ivo?" said Neva angrily. "Why are you doing this?"

"I have my reasons."

"Ridiculous, childish ones!"

"No."

"Your sister is right, Ivo," said Brock. "You should not let Vassek bait you into this. It could be dangerous."

"We'll see."

"Well?" said Vassek. "Have you changed your mind?"

"Why should I change my mind?" said Ivo, and putting his hand on the fence he vaulted over it and walked across the enclosure towards him.

Tarnir, standing next to Vassek, studied him.

"Your name?" he asked.

"Ivo."

"And you are from Nordan?"

"Yes."

"You have no buckler." He beckoned to one of the guards who came into the enclosure and gave his to Ivo.

"Do you know the rules?"

"I'm not sure I do."

"In spite of what just happened, if you are disarmed or wounded or forced out of the ring, the match is over. However, you can also own yourself beaten and yield." He turned to Vassek. "Is that understood?"

Vassek nodded.

"Well, see that you don't forget it," he said sternly and going back to his place beside Jeranus, he gave the signal to begin.

Drawing their swords, Ivo and Vassek saluted the queen and princess and then faced one another. Vassek was smiling again, but his eyes were cold, and now that his anger had left him, Ivo felt a pang of anxiety. He had used his sword only once as far as he could remember—against Harnac the Hilti—and while Liall had told Jartan that he was a good swordsman—and he felt he was—he had no real proof of it. What if they were both wrong? What if Vassek not only beat him but wounded him seriously? For, despite Tarnir's admonition, Ivo knew that he would do so if he could.

Vassek cut at him—a swinging, overhand stroke—and as Ivo raised his buckler and warded it off, his anxiety left him. For he found he did not have to think about what he should do; he did it smoothly, easily and instinctively. Again Vassek cut at him, and again, and both times Ivo fended off his strokes, barely moving. During the previous match, he had seen many openings that Dannus had not seen or had not taken advantage of and he saw others now. But, if he could avoid it, he did not wish to wound Vassek, and so he remained on the defensive, knowing what the next stroke would be before it came and putting it by either with his buckler or his blade.

Vassek was no longer smiling now. He was scowling, and he pressed his attack, striking even harder and more quickly, and at the same time he began moving to his left. Ivo knew what he was doing. By moving towards Ivo's unguarded side he was trying to turn him so that the sun would shine in his eyes. Ivo turned halfway, until he was facing the pavilion, then went over to the attack himself.

Parrying one of Vassek's cuts, he struck back at him, once, twice, three times, then thrust over the top of his buckler, checking his blade at the last moment so that the point barely touched Vassek's throat.

Vassek's eyes widened, and he paled. He recovered, stepped back and tried to take the initiative again, but Ivo did not give him a chance. Again he cut at him, from the right and the left and the right again, and Vassek began to fall back. Ivo followed, pressing him hard, until Vassek reached the woven willow fence. Ivo feinted, and when Vassek raised his buckler, he thrust hard and true. His point struck the centre of the buckler, and Vassek staggered back. The fence caught him just below the hips and, losing his balance, he fell on his back outside the enclosure.

There was a moment of silence, then a roar of laughter from the crowd, followed by cheers and a storm of applause.

Vassek got to his feet, his face crimson.

"I'll kill you for that!" he said fiercely, and he tried to step back into the enclosure, but Tarnir seized him by the arm and stopped him.

"Hold, you fool!" he said. "Don't you know when you've been over-matched? He could have killed you half a dozen times if he wished. Now leave the field!"

Vassek hesitated. Then, sheathing his sword, he stalked off into the crowd. Ivo put up his sword also. He was still facing the pavilion and for the first time he became aware of the fact that the queen, the princess, Jeranus and the warden were all looking at him. Tarnir conferred with Jeranus for a moment, then came towards him.

"That was as fine an exhibition of swordsmanship as I have ever seen," he said. "I declare you the winner of the trial-at-arms and offer you a post with the Queen's Guard. Do you accept?"

Ivo turned. Neva, Liall and Brock were standing where he had left them. And though Neva was no longer pale, he knew that she was still angry. Well, he could not help that. He turned back to Tarnir.

"I am honored," he said. "Yes, I accept."

"Good. Come with me." He led Ivo to the pavilion. "Your Majesty, may I present Ivo of Nordan, the winner of this year's contests, who will serve in your guard."

The queen nodded graciously to him.

"You did very well," she said.

"He did better than well," said Jeranus. "As Tarnir said, it was the best swordsmanship we have ever had here. Who taught you, Ivo?"

This was not the time or place to say he did not

know, so he answered, "My father."

"And who is your father?"

Again he knew he must answer so he gave the first name that occurred to him.

"Jartan."

"Jartan of Nordan." Jeranus shook his head. "I do not know him—which is strange. For I thought I knew every great fighting man, not just here but in Andor. Well, we shall talk again."

"It seemed to me that you did not plan to enter the contest," said the princess, "and would not have if Vassek had not said what he did to you. Is that true?"

"Yes, Your Highness," said Ivo.

"Why was that?"

"Because I was not sure I was good enough."

"So you are not just a fine swordsman. You are modest, too," she said, smiling. "Well, I am glad you did fight him. And I'm glad you won."

"Thank you, Your Highness."

Her father, the Warden, looked sharply at her, then at Ivo.

"Both the count and my daughter had questions for you. I have one, too. Did you come here alone?"

"No, Your Excellency. I did not."

"Who came with you?"

"My sister and a good friend of mine."

"Your sister?" He seemed surprised and a little disappointed.

"Yes."

"What made you ask that, Cadorno?" asked the queen.

"I noticed that he talked to someone before he challenged Vassek. And he glanced over at the far side of the enclosure before he accepted Tarnir's offer to join your guard."

"You are as observant as Devita, brother," said the queen. "Will they stay on here in Mirana, too, Ivo?"

"I do not know, Your Majesty. Since I did not intend to enter the trials but only watch them, we did not discuss it."

"Well, perhaps you should do so now. Call them over."

"Yes, Your Majesty," said Ivo. The crowd was breaking up now, leaving the field, but Neva, Liall and Brock were still there, on the far side of the enclosure. Ivo waved to them, and they began walking around the enclosure towards the pavilion. Then Brock left them, and they came on alone.

The queen watched them. Her face, until now somewhat cold, softened and a strange, almost wistful expression came over it. When they reached the pavilion, Neva dipped low in a reverence and Liall bowed.

"This is my sister, Neva, Your Majesty," said Ivo. "And my friend, Nord."

"You are both from Nordan, too?" said the queen.

"Yes, Your Majesty," said Liall.

"It is many years since I have been there," said the

queen. "I should visit it again for I seem to have underestimated it as did that red-headed trooper Ivo fought. What was his name?"

"Vassek, Your Majesty," said Tarnir.

She nodded, her eyes still on Neva.

"Your brother has agreed to serve in my guard and will be staying on here in Mirana. What will you do?"

"I do not know, Your Majesty," said Neva. "If there is any way I can stay here also, I would like to."

"You are fond of him?"

"Yes, Your Majesty," said Neva simply.

"Your parents would not mind if they lost both of you at once?"

Neva glanced at Ivo. They had not discussed this and she did not know what he had told the queen, but she said, "We have no parents."

"They are both dead?"

"Yes, Your Majesty."

"I am sorry. I do not know which is worse: for children to lose their parents or for a parent to lose a child. I think the latter." Then as the princess put her hand sympathetically on her arm, "What is it, Devita?"

"Nothing, Aunt Galla. Except . . . I have a tiring woman, but couldn't Neva stay on here as my lady-in-waiting?"

"Would you like that, Neva?" asked the queen.

"Yes, Your Majesty."

"So be it." She glanced at Liall. "I suppose you would like to stay on here with your friends."

"If I can, Your Majesty."

"Are you a swordsman, too?"

"Yes, Your Majesty. Not as good as Ivo, but good enough."

"We shall let Tarnir see what he thinks of that. If he is satisfied, you shall be a member of my guard, too." She rose. "I leave Ivo and Nord in your care, Tarnir. And Neva in yours, Devita." And she moved off, followed by Jeranus and her guard.

The warden remained there for a moment.

"So," he said. "We shall now have three from Nordan in the palace."

"Yes, father," said Devita. "You do not object, do you?"

He looked at Ivo, his face expressionless, then at Neva and Liall.

"Why should I object?" he said and he went off after the queen.

Chapter 15

That was your only reason for doing it?" said Neva.

"Yes," said Ivo. "If we want to find the last fragment of the stone, we must stay here. And I knew that if I became one of the Queen's Guards it would not only give us a reason for staying, but it would make it possible for us to do so."

"You had no way of knowing that Liall and I would be able to stay, too."

"I was sure I could arrange it somehow. And I did. What I can't understand is why you were so angry."

"You asked that before and I told you," said Liall. "She was afraid of what might happen if you fought Vassek."

"Were you?" asked Ivo.

"Yes," said Neva. "And I still think it was childish of you to challenge him. That you did it because of the things he said. Because you wanted to show him—and the princess—what a fine swordsman you were!"

"That's ridiculous!" said Ivo. "The idea came to me before I ever saw or even heard of the princess—while we were talking to Jartan!"

They were in Ivo's room in the palace: a large room overlooking the sea. Neva had been given one next to Devita's and had just joined Ivo and Liall.

"If I may say so," said Liall, "this is rather silly. Things have worked out very well—better than we had any right to expect."

"I agree," said Ivo. "Especially if you're accepted for the guard, too. Besides, we have something more important to talk about."

"What's that?"

"Jeranus wanted to know who had taught me to use a sword, and I said my father. He asked me who he was and I had to say something so I said Jartan. But you said our parents were dead."

"So far as we know they are," said Neva.

"Yes, but we should both tell the same story. I suppose the best thing would be to say that while our mother died some time ago, our father died only recently—within the past few months."

"I don't like lying even when it's in a good cause," said Neva.

"Neither do I. But I'm afraid we have no choice."

There was a knock on the door, and Tarnir came in.

"Are you ready?" he asked Liall.

"Yes."

"Then come along. You too, Ivo."

"May I come also?" asked Neva.

"If you like."

He led the way along the corridor, down the stairs and into a small courtyard near the guard room where Jeranus was waiting.

"Will you try him or shall I?" asked Tarnir.

"Why don't we let Ivo do it?" said Jeranus.

"Very well." He went into the guard room, came out with two bucklers and gave one to Ivo and the other to Liall. "Now let's see what you can do, Nord."

Ivo and Liall faced one another and began their match. Since he had no idea how skilled a swordsman Liall was, Ivo had decided to hold back and remain on the defensive. But after the first few passes, he relaxed. Liall was a splendid swordsman—as good as Vassek and perhaps better. Warming to the contest, he went over to the attack and for several minutes they exchanged cuts and thrusts.

"That will do," said Tarnir finally. And turning to Jeranus, "What do you think?"

"Ivo was not pressing him—which is understandable—but it does not matter. He is certainly the equal of anyone now on the guard."

"So I think too," said Tarnir. "As Her Majesty said, we seem to have underestimated Nordan."

"Yes," said Jeranus. He was looking thoughtfully at Ivo. "You say it was your father who taught you to use a sword?"

"Yes, count."

"Strange. I have fought many men and watched many others, not just in the trials-at-arms here but in the wars with Andor. And there is only one man who used his point the way you do. I still bear the scars of my last meeting with him."

"Tharlak?" said Tarnir.

"Yes."

"Who was he?" asked Ivo.

"Andor's war leader, the friend of King Lanis, and probably the greatest swordsman there or in Brunn. But he has been dead for many years."

"My father has been dead for only a few months."

"That is why I say it is strange. Well . . ." He was turning away when the Princess Devita came into the courtyard. "Were you looking for me, Your Highness?"

"Yes. And for Neva. I thought I would find her here. I wondered what you had decided about Nord."

"Tarnir has accepted him for the guard. So he will stay here too."

"I'm delighted to hear that. You and Ivo must be pleased, Neva."

"We are, Your Highness."

"I'm glad. But now I think we should leave them to Tarnir. You will see them both again later."

"Yes, Your Highness."

Ivo and Liall watched them go, then gave their attention to Tarnir while he explained their duties to them. So far as was possible, he would let them stand guard together. But, best of all, they would share Ivo's room, which was what they had hoped for.

They all dined in the great hall that evening, a large vaulted room with windows overlooking the harbor. Neva was at the high table, sitting next to the princess, and Ivo and Liall were at the far end of the cross table with the other members of the guard. They hoped to be able to meet afterwards, but again the princess took Neva off with her and they had no chance to.

The princess and Neva talked until quite late—mostly about Mirana and life at the palace—for which Neva was grateful since she was not anxious to talk about herself. She was about to help Devita get ready for bed when the queen sent for them.

They found her on the balcony outside her chamber, which, like most of the rooms in the palace, overlooked the harbor and the sea beyond.

"I was not sleepy," said the queen, "and I hoped that you were not; that you would sit with me for a while."

"You know that I am always happy to, Aunt Galla," said Devita.

"Yes. You have always been patient with me and my moods—more so than your father—and therefore good for me."

"Father is a man and concerned with other things. But he loves you as much as I do."

"Perhaps." Though it was dark on the balcony Neva sensed that the queen was looking at her rather than Devita and now she spoke to her. "This must all be very strange to you, child. To be living, not just among strangers, but in a place that is very different from the one you have always known."

"It is different, Your Majesty, and it is a little strange. But the princess has been very kind to me, and I am sure I will be happy here."

"I hope you will be. Tell me about Nordan."

"What would you like to know, Your Majesty?"

"I have not been there for many years—not since the king was killed, and I remember it as a small village—small but pretty—set high in the hills."

"It is small, Your Majesty," said Neva carefully. "And it is also pretty."

"Your brother told us a little about your father—at least that he was a swordsman. But what about your mother? What was she like?"

"I don't really know, Your Majesty. She died when I was very young, and I barely remember her."

"Surely your father talked of her."

"Very little. All I know of her is that she was very beautiful and that he loved her very much."

"It is easy to believe that she was beautiful, for you are, too. But who brought you up?"

"Why, our father."

"Just your father?"

"Yes."

"That is not so easy to believe."

"Why do you say that, Aunt Galla?" asked Devita.

"Because men and women are very different—not just physically but in the way they think and talk and feel. Neva has a manner and a grace that she could not have learned from a man."

"Though her father may have brought her up, I am sure that she spent time with other women," said Devita.

"I did, Your Majesty," said Neva.

"While they may have taught her to weave and cook, they could not have taught her the things I am talking about. That requires a certain closeness."

"Why could there not have been a certain woman to whom she felt very close?" said Devita.

"There must have been. And not just an ordinary woman. But why are you so defensive about her, Devita?"

"Because I like her."

"So do I. That is why I am so interested in her. But you also like her brother, do you not?"

"I hardly know him. I have not spoken more than a dozen words to him. But yes. I do like him."

Neva stirred. Though she had known that this

was true, she had not expected Devita to be so honest about it.

"That was clear," said the queen. "Not just to me but to your father, too. You should be careful, Devita."

"Of what?"

"Of liking Ivo too much. Or at least of letting your father know that you do. He has other plans for you."

"I am my own mistress!"

"We would all like to think that, but it is not true. We are none of us entirely our own to command—not even I."

"But that is because you are the queen."

"Which you will be, too one day—if not here then elsewhere."

"But what has that to do with my liking Ivo?"

"Perhaps nothing. Perhaps a great deal. In any case, I thought I should warn you. And now you must both be tired, you particularly, Neva. You can go."

"We will be glad to stay if you would like us to, Your Majesty."

"No. It will be some time before I am ready for bed. I hope you rest well, both of you."

"Thank you, Your Majesty."

"Good night, Aunt Galla," said Devita. She kissed the queen and then she and Neva went back inside, leaving her there on the balcony.

Sometime in the watches of that night a dream came to Neva. It took her from her bed in the room near Devita's and carried her high above the sleeping world to a tall peak which, even in the darkness, she recognized as Tarec. The shattered stone lay as she had last seen it, sombre in the moonlight. And though this time Ivo and Liall were not with her, she was not alone. A figure in a hooded white robe stood at the plateau's eastern edge looking first at Andor, then at Brunn. With a deep feeling of awe, Neva went towards her and made her a reverence for she knew that this was the being whose image had been cut on the stone.

The White Lady did not turn, but it was clear she knew Neva was there.

"My lady, why are you so sorely troubled?" asked Neva.

She spoke to her as she had to Akala, without words, and the White Lady answered in the same way.

"Look."

With eyes more farseeing than Akala's, Neva looked at Andor and wherever she looked, armed men were moving towards Lantar, gathering in the fields and meadows that surrounded it.

"Will they attack soon?"

"Within days, perhaps less."

"What will come of it?"

"Even I cannot tell you that, but I can show you what could come of it."

She gestured, and the waiting army moved north towards Brunn. A great host had gathered there, too, but they were overwhelmed, scattered, and the forces of Andor drove on towards Mirana and east and west, and throughout Brunn there were scenes like the ones embroidered on the tapestry in the room of Liall's mother: cities, towns and villages attacked and burning, dead men lying in the streets and fields, women screaming, children fleeing fatherless and babes abandoned.

But Brunn, as strong as Andor, was not yet beaten. The scattered forces rallied, drove out the invaders and followed them into Andor. And now the same bloody scenes were repeated there; burning cities and farmsteads, fields laid waste, and cattle wandering with none to tend them. Back and forth moved the red tide of war, and as those who fought became fewer, they became even more savage, killing more and more wantonly until all, both north and south, was a waste and a devastation. Then, in an exhausted pause, a dark figure came forward, promising peace, and mounted to power over both Andor and Brunn. But though his words had been soft and honeyed, Neva sensed that it was he who had loosed the evil that had swept both lands and that he was even more ruthless than all those who had slain and burned. And though she tried to see his face, she could not for it was turned from her. But on his shoulder, whispering in his ear, was the gore-crow.

"Who is he?" she asked.

"His name means nothing," said the White Lady. "He is but one finger of a far greater hand; a hand that first reached out of the darkness when time began. It is what this triumph would mean that brought me here."

"There cannot be more!" said Neva.

"Look up."

Neva looked up and now she saw with the White Lady's eyes: saw other worlds above and beyond and around, as many world as there were stars. And each was poised in an exact balance, part light, part dark. And as the world beneath her tipped slowly down and darkness flooded it, so each of the other worlds moved and turned that much farther from the light.

Her senses numbed, Neva looked again at the dark figure on the throne beneath her.

"And can you do nothing to stop him?"

"Though he is mortal and I am not, I am as bound by the laws that govern the great balance as he is. I have loved, protected and instructed. I can do no more unless—in pride or desperation—he go beyond the laws by using powers that are forbidden."

"Is all lost then?"

"Not yet. Not while a single spark of light remains anywhere."

The White Lady turned now, and for the first time Neva saw her face; saw and knew it.

"You will forget what you have seen," she said, "as you have forgotten many other things. But it is my hope that because I showed you what I did, the spark will live on in you even if the time of the great darkness comes."

Chapter 16

Ivo had been sleeping fitfully and uneasily also. Finally he woke, got out of bed and went to the window. He was peering up at the stars that were becoming dimmer with the approach of dawn when Liall sat up with a start.

"What is it?" he asked.

"Nothing. I had a bad dream."

"What kind of dream?"

"About a dark cloud. It was very small at first but it became larger and larger until it shadowed everything—not just the palace here but all of Brunn and Andor."

"And you were looking for it?"

"Yes."

"I did not think of you as someone who believed in dreams."

"I don't know if I believe in them or not. But I did see something."

"What?"

"Not a cloud or a shadow but a bird."

"A gull?"

"No. It was too dark to be certain, but I thought it was the gore-crow that we first saw on Tarec and then on the heath."

"That's impossible. What would it be doing here?"

"What was it doing on the heath?"

"We thought it was following us, spying on us."

"Yes."

"I still think, if it was anything, it was a gull."

"Don't you think I can tell the difference between a gull and a crow?"

"In the dark?"

Ivo hesitated. "Perhaps not."

He went back to bed for a while, but did not sleep. Then he and Liall dressed in the uniforms they had been given—blue tunics blazoned with the sea-serpent of Brunn—and went down to the great hall. They broke their fast with the other members of the guard and were about to report for duty when Neva came into the hall.

"Good morning, Neva," said Liall. "Did you sleep well?"

"Well enough until just before dawn."

"What happened then?"

"Something woke me. I went to the window and there on the balcony railing was the gore-crow we saw on Tarec and on the heath. I don't know how long it had been there, but when I came to the window it flew off."

"Which way did it fly?"

"South. Back towards Andor."

Liall nodded, looking thoughtful, and Ivo found it interesting that though Liall had argued with him, he had not argued with Neva.

"I saw it also," he said. "You think it followed us?"

"Probably. In any case, now it knows we are here."

"Well, there's nothing we can do about it." He rose. "We must go now and report to Tarnir."

"Not this morning."

"Why not?"

"Because I have just seen him. The princess is going down to the quays and she asked that the two of you be permitted to attend her."

"Oh. Just the princess?"

"No. I will be going, too."

"That sounds more promising than guard duty," said Ivo. "Shall we go now?"

"Yes. We should not keep her waiting."

They left the great hall, and in a few moments Devita came down the wide curving stairs. She was wearing a pale yellow gown, and a silver fillet held her long dark hair in place.

"Neva has told you where we are going?"

"Yes, Your Highness," said Ivo.

"There are things I wish to do, and since you do not know Mirana I thought I would be your guide and show you the sights."

She led the way out of the palace and down a steep, cobbled street that clung to the side of the cliff. Houses, painted white but with brightly colored doors, were built against the cliff. On the other side was a stone parapet over which they could see the harbor, the breakwater that protected it, and the blue sea beyond. Gulls and terns wheeled and soared overhead and the air had a keen, fresh tang to it.

Housewives, returning from market with their baskets or standing in their doorways, greeted the princess with easy and familiar warmth, and she responded graciously, calling many of them by name.

Down below all was bustle. Shops, booths and stands lined the landward side of the broad avenue that ran along the waterfront. On the other side were the quays where the ships were tied up; long, low merchant vessels with sea-serpent prows and smaller, beamy fishing boats, all with their sails furled, huddled together like resting sea-birds.

Tradesmen and craftsmen hawking their wares, baggy trousered seamen and porters carrying baskets, boxes and bales all greeted the princess also and she responded to them as she had to the women with a smile or a nod.

"Why do you not walk with me?" she asked Ivo, who had been following a few paces behind her with Neva and Liall.

"Because I did not think it was proper."

"It is quite proper. Besides, how can I talk to you if you are not at my side?"

"I did not realize that you wished to talk to me."

"Did I not say I would be your guide?"

"Yes, Princess," he said and lengthening his stride he began walking next to her.

"What do you think of all this?" asked Devita.

"It is all new and quite wonderful, Princess. Not just the shops and ships and people, but the sea, too."

"You have never seen it before?"

"No, Princess."

"I did not think there was anyone in Brunn who did not know the sea. Well, I will tell you about it—where our ships go, what they take and bring back. But some day you must tell me about Nordan."

"Yes, Princess."

Liall, walking behind them with Neva, glanced at her and said, "You should not look that way, Neva."

"What way?"

"Half hurt, half angry. I know that you and Ivo are very close but you cannot expect to be with him forever. One day he will marry and leave you."

"Will he?" she said with bitter irony. "It is thoughtful of you to warn me."

They paused, waiting in the warm sun as the princess went into one of the shops, talked to the merchant and came out with two long, intricately dyed scarfs.

"Do you like these, Neva?"

"They're beautiful, Princess."

"I think so, too. It's why I came down here today. They are from the Kyrkian Islands where they weave the finest silk in the world and dye it with a dye from shellfish. Which do you like best?"

"I like them both, but I think the blue one would be more becoming to you."

"It was not myself I was thinking of. It was you. And I think the green one would go best with your eyes and hair. Here."

"You mean it is for me?"

"Of course."

"Thank you, Princess. I will always treasure it—not just because it is beautiful but because you gave it to me."

"You turn phrases like a courtier," said Devita, smiling. "I thought we were friends."

"We are."

"Then say no more about it. There are few things as pleasant as being able to give something to someone one likes."

"Very well, Princess," said Neva and she draped the scarf over her shoulders.

The merchant came out of the shop, and Devita paid him and they went on again. A crowd had gathered a short distance ahead of them, near one of the quays. There were tradesmen in it and artisans and seamen but at the centre were two elderly men; one wearing the rich robe of a merchant and the other a sea captain's boots and cape. As they drew near, the merchant turned away angrily and pushed his way through the crowd.

"You seem troubled, Fornar," said Devita.

"Not troubled, Princess, furious!" said the merchant. "Timak has just returned from Oralia, and do you know what he is asking for silver? Double what he asked last year!"

"It is a long voyage to Oralia."

"It is no longer now than it was then. He asks it because he thinks I will pay it. But I told him I will not. I have been a silversmith for almost two score years. I made that fillet you are wearing, your father's chain of office and the cup out of which the queen drinks. But I will give away my tools and let my forge grow cold before I will pay what he asks!"

"I have heard much the same thing from others," said Devita. "At the same time the fishermen say that it is scarcely worth their while to cast their nets. But what is to be done about it?"

"I am not of the court, Princess. I know nothing of high policy. But I know that there is silver, gold and iron there," he pointed south, "in the mountains of Andor, much nearer at hand than Oralia or any of the islands of the sea."

"Are you saying that we should attack Andor, con-

Chadron State College Library
Chadron, Nebraska

quer it and take what we want?"

"No, Princess. One of the reasons you are so well loved is because you have always come among us and we have been able to talk to you. And so let me remind you that there was a time—short it is true—when we got many things we needed for a fair price from Andor, and we—and the fishermen, too—had a better market for our goods than we have ever had before or since."

"During the time of the truce, you mean. But that was before the great betrayal."

"Yes, the great betrayal," said the silversmith sombrely. "I know what the queen suffered as a result of it. But I wonder if she and your father have ever thought of how costly it has been for us, too." And he moved off towards his shop.

Devita looked after him unhappily, then turned to Neva, Ivo and Liall.

"This is why I come down here so often," she said. "So that those who cannot speak to the queen or my father can talk to me. And it is also why I am reluctant to come. For each day more and more of them speak as Fornar did. Is it the same in Nordan?"

"We know even less of high policy than those here in Mirana," said Liall carefully. "But we have heard some talk about the way things are. Is there nothing that can be done about it?"

"I do not know since I know little about the truce—it ended about the time that I was born. On the other hand, I have lived with the tale of the great betrayal. It was, in fact, my father who warned the king and queen about it."

"How could he do that?" asked Neva.

"He has been a hard and bitter man since my mother died. But he is also wise, and he has always been able to read signs. And there was one about that time that he felt was very significant."

"What sign was that?"

"The royal falconer came to court one day shortly before the betrayal with a strange tale. He had been on Tarec, a mountain in the far west between Andor and Brunn, seeking an eaglet. Though few go there, Ima's priestesses have always said that when Ima founded Brunn she set up a black stone there. The falconer—his name was Largar—said that he had seen the stone and that while he was there a lightning bolt struck and shattered it. He was very concerned about it and so was my father. He said it was an omen that the truce would be broken too. And of course he was right."

"Falconers are great tellers of tales," said Liall with pretended casualness.

"They are. And Largar told me many when I was little," said Devita. "But I still believe that this one was true. He was not against peace with Andor as some here were. And besides he brought a fragment of the stone back with him as proof of what he'd said."

Ivo hesitated, afraid to ask the next and most important question, but Neva was not.

"What became of it?" she asked.

"The king, my uncle, gave it to Ima's priestesses, and they put it in her temple. It is still there."

"I would like to see it," said Neva.

"It is only a small piece of black stone. But you should see the temple. I will take you there."

She led them along the quays to a promontory that formed the western side of the harbor. On it was a white, many columned building. They went into it. It was open on all sides except the far end where a statue stood on a block of marble. The statue was tall—as tall as a tall woman—and clearly very old, for it was crudely carved with the features barely suggested. But perhaps because of its simplicity it was very beautiful and filled the temple with its presence.

Devita bowed her head reverently and so did Neva, Ivo and Liall, and then they approached it. On the block of marble in front of the statue was a fragment of black stone slightly larger than the one the gorecrow had taken, the one that Zothar had shown them. And like it, there were characters inscribed upon one side.

"May I have your sword, Ivo?" asked Neva.

He gave it to her, and she held it in front of the stone fragment and looked into it as she had on the top of Tarec.

"Well?" said Liall.

"The last two words are 'Kennar's son,' " she said.

She gave Ivo back his sword, and the three of them looked at one another.

"I think I understand now," said Ivo.

"Yes," said Liall, soberly and unhappily.

"What do you understand?" asked Devita. She had stepped back, startled, when Ivo had drawn his sword, and now she was studying them. They did not answer immediately, and she frowned. "From the time I first saw all of you at the trial-at-arms, I had a strange feeling about you. Who are you and from whence do you come?"

"I think we should tell her," said Neva. And when Ivo and Liall nodded, "We are not from Nordan, Princess."

"So I was beginning to suspect. And I repeat, who are you and what do you here?"

"We will tell you if you will tell us something. Are you happy at the way things are now? At the hatred of Andor and the skirmishing along the border that threatens to become open and bloody war?"

"You must know that I am not."

"So we thought. And therefore we will tell you that we are here because we do not like it either and were seeking a way to put an end to it and bring peace to Brunn and Andor."

"You said *were* seeking. Does that mean you have found a way?"

"We think so. Though we did not say so, we knew

about the black stone that had been set up on Tarec before you mentioned it. In fact, we have been on Tarec and seen it. Because we were told that the answer we were looking for was written on it."

"And was it there?"

"Not all of it. Two pieces of the stone—and of the inscription—were missing. We found one of the missing fragments in Andor. This is the other. And now we know how what we want can be accomplished."

"And will you tell me?"

"We will tell you what the inscription said. It was written in the old Tree alphabet and written in a way that made it difficult to decipher. But it reads: 'Andor and Brunn shall again be one when Ima's daughter marries Kennar's son.' "

"I do not understand," said Devita. "Who is Kennar's son?"

"Who is Ima's daughter?" asked Neva.

"I'm not sure. I suppose, since Ima founded Brunn and in time I will rule it, that I might be considered her daughter."

"Yes," said Neva. "And since those in Andor believe that it was founded by Kennar, Prince Liall who will rule there one day would be Kennar's son."

"Then what you are saying is that if I truly wish to bring peace then I must marry him."

"It is not we who say it. That is what was written on the stone."

"But I know nothing about Prince Liall beyond his

name And besides . . ." She broke off.

"Yes, Princess?"

She looked at each of them in turn, her eyes troubled.

"You have told me much. And still it is my feeling that you have not told me all."

"That is true, Princess. We have not."

"Well, I do not want to hear anymore. Not now. I must think about what you have said already. Let us go back to the palace."

They left the temple in silence, and in silence went back along the quays and up to the palace. When they were at the foot of the stairs, Neva, who had been walking behind the princess with Ivo and Liall, came forward tentatively, but Devita stopped her.

"No, Neva," she said. "I will send for you if I have anything to say to you."

And she went up the stairs alone.

Chapter 17

There was no word or sign from the princess until late in the afternoon. She did not come down to the great hall for the midday meal, and Neva, Ivo and Liall were out in the terraced gardens when one of the palace servants came along the winding path and spoke briefly to Neva. When he left, she rejoined Ivo and Liall.

"She has asked me to come to her chamber," she said. "You are to come, too."

"What do you think she will say?" asked Liall.

"I don't know."

As they entered the palace, Devita's father, the warden, came down the stairs.

"Ah, the three from Nordan," he said, looking at

them sharply and searchingly. "I thought you were with the princess."

"We were this morning," said Neva. "And we are going to join her now."

"Where is she?"

"In her chamber."

Nodding, he strode off and they went up the stairs. Neva knocked, and when the princess answered, they went in. Devita was at the window, her eyes still troubled.

"You have given me a difficult problem," she said. "More difficult than you know."

"We're sorry, Princess," said Neva.

"I'm sure it was not by choice. I would do much to bring peace to Brunn. I have always thought I would do anything, but . . ." She broke off. "There is something you have not told me yet."

"Yes, Princess."

"I was not ready to hear it before. But now I must. What is it?"

"When we told you what was written on the stone, you said you knew nothing of Prince Liall besides his name. That is not true. Nord is Prince Liall."

"So I suspected," said Devita. She looked at Liall. "You have risked a great deal by coming here; your freedom and possibly even your life."

"Yes, Princess."

"Did you know what would be required of you before you came?"

"If you mean what must be done to put an end to the hatred between Andor and Brunn, no, Princess. None of us knew that before we read what was on the stone fragment in Ima's temple."

"And if you had known, would you have come?"

"Why do you ask that?"

"Because I cannot help wondering about it." She looked at him levelly. "If you were free to choose whom you would to marry, would you have chosen me?"

He flushed slightly. "That is not a fair question. How often can a prince marry whom he would?"

"Not often. Nor a princess either. Well, you have answered me."

"Princess . . ." he began.

"Nay. Say no more." Then, as someone knocked on the door, "Enter."

A servant came in with a tray and set it down on a bench. There were some small cakes on it and four silver cups, one of them elaborately chased and jewelled.

"Thank you, Bahri," she said. The servant bowed and left.

"I have eaten nothing since early this morning," she said, picking up one of the cakes and the jewelled cup. "I asked for wine from Weststrand, which is our best, and I thought you might like some, too."

"You are very kind, Princess," said Liall. He took one of the other cups and was raising it to his lips when Neva said, "No, Liall. Don't!"

"What?" He looked at her, startled.

"I said, don't!"

She had one of the plain silver cups in her hand, too, and though she had not tasted it, she had smelled it. Now she set it down again.

"But why?"

"Yes, why?" asked Devita. She sipped the wine in the jewelled cup. "Do you think it has gone bad?"

"No, Princess."

"Then why? . . ." She stiffened and her eyes flashed. "You think there is something in it. Venom perhaps!"

"Yes, Princess," said Neva steadily.

"Give me the cup!" she said angrily and taking it from Liall she was about to drink it herself when Ivo struck it from her hand.

"Don't, Princess!"

"You mean you think it is envenomed, too?"

"Yes, Princess. Not yours, but these others."

"And I say it is impossible!"

"Let us see," said Neva. There was a mimosa in the corner of the room, the kind that is sometimes called a sensitive plant. She emptied her cup over it, and at once its leaves curled up and it began to droop. Devita stared at it.

"I still say it cannot be! If it's true, who could have done it?"

"Not you, Princess," said Neva. "That we know."

"But then, who? . . ." She went to the door, opened it and called, "Bahri!"

"Yes, Princess?" said the serving man, coming in.

"We think there may be something wrong with the wine. Did you draw it yourself?"

"Yes, Princess."

"And brought it here directly?"

"No, Princess. I was on my way when I met your father. He asked me where I was going, and when I told him, he said I should first take a message to the Count Jeranus for him."

"And did you?"

"Yes, Princess. I left the tray in the great hall and went to give the count his message. Then I brought the tray here."

"I see."

"Shall I bring you other wine?"

"No, Bahri." Then when he was gone, "My father. It could not have been he!" She looked at all three of them in turn, and none of them said anything. "You think it was he, don't you? But why? How could he know who you were or why you were here?"

"You said he could read signs," said Neva. "And you also said you had a strange feeling about us yourself. Perhaps he guessed."

"Perhaps. And he has always been against any move that might mean peace with Andor. But to do anything like this! . . ." She looked again at the mimosa whose leaves were now turning brown, and then at Liall. "Very well," she said with sudden resolution, "If it will accomplish what you say—or what the stone says—I will marry you."

"I am honored, Princess," said Liall. "And I honor you for your gallantry. For I think that if you could give your heart where you would, it would not be to me."

"It is no easier for you than it is for me. You love Neva, do you not?"

"Yes, Princess," he said simply. "I have since I first saw her."

"Please, Liall . . ." said Neva.

"Let him say it," said Devita. "If he has never said it before, it is good that it should be said now. As for me . . ." She looked at Liall. "Ah, well. It does not matter. What we should talk about is how we can do what we must do. The priestesses at the temple are my friends, and it may be that they would marry us secretly."

"That will not do," said Neva.

"Why not?"

"Because it is too dangerous. If your father has guessed who we are and what we would do—and if it was he who tried to kill us—he will try again. You must be married openly—with all in both Brunn and Andor accepting it."

"Then it cannot be done," said Devita. "In spite of what I said this morning, there are too many here who are opposed to peace with Andor—not just my father and the queen—but others, too. And we have very little time. For I fear that any day now we may be at war."

"So I think, too," said Liall. "The king, my uncle, seemed determined on it before we left Andor. Is there nothing we can do, then?"

"There may be something," said Neva slowly, "though it will be difficult and dangerous."

"What is that?" asked Ivo.

She told them, and they were silent for several minutes.

"What you said is true," said Liall. "Many things could go wrong, but I think we should attempt it. Are we agreed?" They nodded. "Since the time is so short, I should go at once."

"I will help you leave the palace," said Devita.

"If you will do that, I think I can do the rest," said Liall. He turned to Neva and Ivo. "I will not say goodbye. We will see one another again."

"I hope we shall," said Ivo. "At least once more."

Liall nodded, and when Devita opened the door, he looked a last time at Neva, then followed the princess out.

"Devita was right," said Ivo. "It was good that it was finally said."

"That Liall loved me?"

"Yes. Did you know it?"

"Of course."

He nodded. "If I knew it, I thought you must. And do you love him?"

"As a friend—a very good friend—yes. But in no other way."

"Why not? He's handsome, brave, thinks much of others, and he is a prince."

She looked at him. "Do you love Devita?" she asked.

"No."

"Why not? She's beautiful, also thinks much of others, and she is a princess."

"I know. And I like and admire her. But I do not love her."

"Then you should understand why I feel as I do about Liall."

"Yes, I suppose I do. About the warden, you said he could have guessed who we were and why we were here. But there is another way he could have known."

"The gore-crow?"

"Yes. We thought it had come here to spy on us, but it might be that it told him, warned him."

"That could well be."

"But what will he do when he discovers we did not drink the wine?"

"He will have to be careful. He cannot let anyone know what he attempted. But he will probably try again."

"Then we must be careful, too."

"Yes." Then suddenly, passionately, "Is there to be

no end to this? Why was this task given to us?"

"I thought you believed there was a compelling reason for it as there was for the spell that was put on us. That they were part of some pattern that in time we would understand."

"And when will that time be? It was as much the spell as the task that took us to Tarec, to Andor and now here. And what have we accomplished? We still know no more about ourselves than when we found ourselves on the heath!"

"I think we have done a great deal. For while we may know nothing more about ourselves than we did, we know that the task is a great one and well worth completing, no matter what the dangers."

"You may know that, but I am not sure I do!"

"Neva . . ." He moved towards her to comfort her, but she drew back.

"No. Don't!"

"I'm sorry."

"I'm the one who's sorry," she said and going to the window, she stood there looking out bleakly.

Devita led Liall along the corridor, down a narrow stair at the far end of it and through little used passages to the stables.

"I am sending Nord on an errand," she said to one of the grooms. "Saddle his horse."

"Yes, Your Highness," he said and went off.

"Princess . . ." Liall began.

"I forced you to say what you did about Neva. But

there is nothing you need say to me."

"Perhaps nothing I need say, but much I would like to say."

"But, being honest, cannot bring yourself to say?"

"On the contrary," he said, looking at her steadily. "It would come very easily to my tongue. I would tell you how beautiful I think you are and how much I admire you for your goodness and your courage. And I would then go on to other things."

"Telling me how much you love me?"

"Telling you how much I think I *can* love you. But I do not think this is the time for it nor a stable the place."

"No, it is not. But at the proper time and in a more fitting place, I will be glad to hear it."

The groom brought out his horse and dropping to one knee Liall kissed her hand.

"Farewell, Princess."

"May you and your mission fare well for all our sakes."

Liall mounted and rode out of the stable. Devita watched him go, and her face was less strained than it had been since she left the temple that morning.

Neva and Ivo looked at her inquiringly when she returned to her chamber.

"He has gone," she said.

"And no one questioned him?" asked Ivo.

"No."

"Tarnir was here a moment ago," said Neva. "The

queen wishes you to attend her in the council chamber."

"Did he say why?"

"No."

"Something is afoot," she said. "You had better come with me."

"The queen will not object?" asked Ivo.

"I don't care if she does."

They followed her down the stairs to the council chamber which was next to the great hall. The two guards outside the door saluted her and looked curiously at Neva and Ivo but said nothing. One of them opened the door and they went in.

The queen sat in a throne at the far end of the room, the warden on one side of her and Count Jeranus on the other. The warden's eyes widened when he saw Neva and Ivo, but he said nothing.

"We have been waiting for you, Devita," said the queen. Then with a frown, "Why have you brought Neva and Ivo with you?"

"Because they are my friends."

"And what about the third from Nordan?" asked the warden. "Is he not a friend, too?"

"Yes, father," said Devita. "But I sent him on an errand."

"What errand?"

"Does it matter?"

"You are acting very strangely, Devita," he said coldly. "The queen summoned you because she had something of great import to tell you. And for you to bring others here with you . . ."

"They and everyone else in Mirana will hear of it soon enough," said the queen. "Why should they not hear it now?" Then turning back to Devita, "Word has been brought to us that Andor's army is massing along the border. There have already been some skirmishes. I have ordered Count Jeranus to muster as great a force as he can as quickly as he can. While the levy will not be complete by morning, it will be large enough so that we can ride south, attack and at long last utterly destroy Andor!"

Chapter 18

The sun was almost directly overhead as they approached the forest. Tarnir and the guard rode in the van, in front of and surrounding the queen, who had the Count Jeranus on one side of her and the warden on the other. Behind them were Devita, Neva and Ivo and behind them, stretching far back across the grassy plain were the armed horsemen of Brunn.

There had been angry words that morning when the warden discovered that Devita intended to ride to the scene of the battle. But the queen intervened, saying that if the battle was lost there would be no safety for anyone, queen or princess, anywhere in Brunn. And since she was going, there was no reason why Devita should not go, too.

Jeranus drew rein on a knoll.

"I do not think you should go any farther, Your Majesty," he said.

"Why not?"

He pointed. Somewhat to their right the green wall of the forest ended in an open area that was dotted with charred tree stumps, the Burnt Place. Beyond it metal glittered, the weapons and bucklers of the hosts of Andor, drawn up in ranks and waiting.

The queen looked, not at her enemies, but at the scorched and blasted ground in front of her.

"This is the place of treachery where my daughter died, is it not?"

Jeranus nodded.

"And so by accident or design it will all end where it began. For this is where we shall join battle with them." She raised her eyes now, dark, burning eyes, looking at Andor's armed might. "Very well, Jeranus. Ima be with you for it is in your hands now."

Ivo glanced at Neva and Devita, then sent his horse forward, drawing up in front of the queen.

"Your Majesty, though I have done naught to deserve it, I ask a boon of you."

"Of all times, I cannot think of a worse one than this," she said, frowning, "when the fate of Brunn is at hazard. But what is the boon?"

"I ask leave, before the battle begins, to meet some champion of Andor in single combat."

"It is a strange request," said the queen.

"It is a ridiculous one," said the Warden. "What purpose will it serve?"

"I do not know," said the queen. "What think you, Jeranus?"

"It is a custom that is not unknown," said the count. "I once met Tharlak, Andor's great captain, and exchanged hand-strokes with him before a battle. And if they agree to it, it will give us time to bring up the rest of our forces."

"Then you would say yes?"

"I see nothing wrong with a challenge, and there is something to be gained by it. But if Andor accepts, it is I who should meet their champion."

"Then I am opposed to it," said the queen. "If anything should happen to you who would lead us in battle?"

"Thank you, Your Majesty," said Ivo. "Count, you have seen me at sword play. Can you fault me there?"

"No, Ivo," said Jeranus. "Though it is not easy for me to say it, I think you could well best me at it."

"Then may I stand forth for Brunn, Your Majesty?"

Still frowning, the queen studied him, then turned to Devita who had joined them as had Neva and Tarnir.

"He is your friend, Devita. What say you?"

"I think he should be permitted to do it."

"Even though you do not know who he will face or what will happen to him?"

"We do not know what will happen to any of us before this day is done."

"That is true. Very well. Tarnir, you have heard what was said. Ride on as our herald and issue the challenge."

"Yes, Your Majesty," said Tarnir, and raising a white scarf as a sign of truce, he cantered forward across the Burnt Place towards the army of Andor.

They waited as a single horseman rode forward to meet him, conferred with him and rode back.

"Think you that the king is there?" asked the queen.

"They are too far off to be certain," said Jeranus. "But I think it is likely."

Finally the horseman joined Tarnir again, and he returned.

"They have agreed to it," he said. "The meeting will take place there." He pointed to the centre of the Burnt Place. "The armies are to remain where they are, but the guard may ride forward with you, Your Majesty, if you would watch."

"I do not like it," said the warden. "Why should we trust Andor more now than we ever have?"

"In this you can trust them," said Jeranus. "Whatever else they me be, they are not truce-breakers."

"Say you so here of all places?"

Jeranus was silent, but the queen said, "Still I will trust them." She looked at the warden. "Fear not, brother. What happens now in this meeting will change nothing. I can live no longer with that which has been between Andor and Brunn as Brunn itself cannot. And for well or ill, it will end today."

"You had best make ready, Ivo," said Jeranus.

"Yes, count," said Ivo.

Taking his war helmet from his saddle bow, he put it on, the nose guard and cheek pieces covering most of his face. Then he rode forward to the edge of the Burnt Place and dismounted. On the far side of the Burnt Place a group of horsemen from Andor were advancing also. Among them Ivo recognized King Lanis, Zothar, and Gildas who had brought them to Lantar from the Mendir Marshes.

Jeranus, the warden, Neva and Devita dismounted, too. Ivo gave his horse's reins to the count, saluted the queen, and Devita, then turned to Neva. Her eyes were large and shadowed.

"May the powers that have been with us this far be with you now," she whispered.

He kissed her, then sword in hand, walked forward to the centre of the seared and scorched area.

A single warrior of Andor had come forward also. Like Ivo, a war helmet covered most of his face, his sword was in his hand and his buckler was ready. They met near the charred stump of a large tree and stood there for a moment, waiting.

Gildar and Tarnir both raised their war-horns and blew a harsh blast, a second and a third, the signal to begin. As the echoes of the last call died away, Ivo dropped his sword and buckler and whipped off his helmet. The warrior who stood opposite him did the same, and they embraced.

There was a gasp from all who watched. Then as Ivo and the champion from Andor stepped back and the queen saw that it was Liall, she said, "What does this mean?"

"Your Majesty," said Ivo, "you said that what happened here at this meeting would change nothing. I pray that it may not be so. For indeed that which has been between Andor and Brunn should end today, but end this way."

"Are you calling for peace—and calling for it here in the very place where my daughter died as a result of Andor's treachery?"

"If there was treachery, it was not on our side but on yours!" said King Lanis. "For it was here that my son died, too!"

"You are mistaken, Your Majesty," said a voice behind Ivo. "And so is the queen."

Ivo and Liall both turned. Jartan had come out of that part of the forest that bordered the Burnt Place and was walking towards them. And in his outstretched hands he held two small gold crowns.

"Tharlak!" said the king.

"More treachery!" said the warden. "Here is the great betrayer himself!"

"Was I the great betrayer," asked Jartan. "Or was it someone else?"

Pulling a dagger from his belt, the warden leaped forward and stabbed Jartan in the breast. There was a ring of steel on steel and Jartan staggered back. But the byrnie he wore under his tunic had turned the blow. Recovering, the warden raised his dagger again to strike at Jartan's unprotected throat, but Ivo seized his wrist and wrested it from him.

"Thank you, Ivo," said Jartan. "I ask you again, Cadorno, was I the betrayer or was it someone else?"

The warden hesitated, his face white. Then, drawing back, "Zothar!" he cried.

Andor's high steward, standing near the king, stirred.

"Why do you call on me?" he asked.

"Why indeed?" said another voice, one that was low and musical. And now Mistress Silvia came out of the forest also. And as she advanced towards them, tall and beautiful in her shimmering grey robe, all that Neva and Ivo had forgotten came back to them.

"So you have decided to play a part in this, too," said Zothar.

"I have played a part in it from the beginninng," said Mistress Silvia. "And now we have come to the end. How stand the sands in your glass, Zothar? Have they not run out?"

"No, not yet!" said Zothar. And taking a short ivory wand from under his robe he pointed it at her. There was a clap of thunder high overhead and a lightning bolt flashed down towards her. She raised her hand,

and at the last moment the bolt was turned aside and struck the scorched earth close to where the warden was standing. He swayed, then fell forward on his face and lay still.

"You should not have done that, Zothar," she said. "For you know that once you use the black arts to gain your ends, you free me to use my powers too. Or are you challenging me?"

"Yes!" said Zothar. "Vendraka, stand by me!"

There was a flutter of wings above them, and the gore-crow came swooping down and settled on a charred tree stump near him. Zothar drew himself up, his eyes blazing. He lifted his wand again and suddenly he was gone. In his place was an enormous serpent, its thick body plated with scales, its mouth agape and its fangs dripping with venom.

Coiling, the serpent struck at Mistress Silvia. But as it did, she held up her hand, palm outward, and the triangular head was checked as if it had struck an invisible shield. Again it struck, writhing closer, and again her outstretched hand held it off. Then she brought her hand down in a sweeping gesture, and the monstrous serpent shuddered and drew back. At the same time it began to change. Its scales lost their color, and it became smaller. It shrank quickly; to the size of a jungle river snake, to that of a viper, then to that of a common grass snake. And still it shrank.

The gore-crow, sitting on the stump, watched with beady eyes. Then, when the snake was no longer than a man's hand, it hopped down, took it in its beak and swallowed it and then flapped off, disappearing into the blue sky to the west.

Ivo let out his held breath with a sigh. King Lanis was the first to speak.

"My lady," he said. "Who are you?"

"I have many names," she said. "Ivo and Neva know one of them."

"We called her Mistress Silvia," said Ivo, "as we called Tharlak, Jartan."

"There is much I do not understand," said the king. "Though I knew it not, it seems Zothar was a warlock."

"Of great powers," said Mistress Silvia. "While his father was your steward and he was young, he studied the dark arts and became a master of them."

"To what end? As far as I know, until just now he never used them."

"He could not use them to gain his wish—which was to rule, not merely Andor but Brunn as well. For there are laws that forbid higher powers, black or white, from using magic to interfere in the affairs of men. But what he did was make a pact with the dark forces. He would have their aid for a period of time, measured in an hour glass he was given, to bring about the destruction of both kingdoms. If he succeeded, he would become master of all between the mountains and the sea. If he failed, he would pay as he did, with his life and more than his life."

"And my brother, the warden?" asked the queen.

"Evil can always find an ally. Your brother was no more content to be merely warden than Zothar was to be high steward. He must have been offered something he wanted to aid Zothar in his plots—perhaps to rule Brunn under him."

"Much of this I can accept," said the king. "I can see how a forked tongue that talks peace but stirs up hatred can accomplish as much as the black arts. But there was a reason for that hatred—on my part at least."

"Only on yours?" said the queen savagely. "Who was it that first proposed peace and an exchange of hostages and then ordered a treacherous assault that cost my daughter her life?"

"I gave no such order!" said the king.

"No, sire, you did not," said Jartan. "But you sent Zothar to oversee the exchange with me. It was he, in concert with the warden, who by trickery and false report caused the fighting to begin here. But surely you have guessed by now that neither Prince Halidar nor Princess Varena are dead."

"Not dead?" said the queen.

"No, Your Majesty. I was wounded in the fighting. But in the darkness and confusion—for torches had fired the encampment—I escaped into the forest with both children. There they remained until a few short weeks ago, protected by Mistress Silvia."

"My lady, is this true?" asked the king.

"It is true," said Mistress Silvia. "Jartan holds their crowns. But did your heart tell you nothing when you first saw Ivo?"

"How could it tell me that which I could not believe? Seeing him so much like what I had hoped my son might be only sharpened my anguish and my anger. Even now I cannot credit it."

"You can credit it," said Mistress Silvia. "And you, too, O Queen."

"I do," said the queen in an unsteady voice. Then turning to Neva and holding out her arms, "Daughter . . ."

That much Ivo saw and no more, for then he was embracing the king and his eyes were dim with tears.

It was later. The armies had drawn back. The warden's body had been removed, and Devita, out of a sense of filial duty if no longer out of love, had accompanied it back to Mirana. Only a few remained in the Burnt Place: the king and queen, Neva and Ivo, Liall, Jartan and Jeranus. And Mistress Silvia. Much had been said.

"And yet," observed the king, "much still remains to be said and done. But one thing above all. How can we ensure that that which has been shall never happen again?"

"Neva and Ivo know," said Mistress Silvia. "I call them that rather than by their true names for so I called them for many years. Ask them."

Ivo looked at Neva who was standing beside the

queen, and when she dropped her eyes, a great shyness came over him too and neither spoke.

"If they will not answer perhaps Liall will tell you. For he knows, too."

"I and also Devita," said Liall. "For she was with us when we read the last of what was written on the shattered stone."

"And what was that?" asked the queen.

" 'Andor and Brunn shall again be one,' " said Liall, " 'when Ima's daughter marries Kennar's son.' "

"Of course," said the king. "What could be simpler? It would seem then that it has little to do with us, Your Majesty."

"Perhaps that is best," said the queen. She looked at Neva. "Have you nothing to say, child?"

"What is there to say?" asked Neva in a low voice. Then color came to her cheeks for Ivo was walking towards her. And when he held out his hand to her she took it.